# REACHING PAST GOODBYE

BILL JACK

Chapbook Press

Schuler Books
2660 28th Street SE
Grand Rapids, MI 49512
(616) 942-7330
www.schulerbooks.com

ISBN 13: 9781943359233

Library of Congress Control Number: 2015959527

Copyright © 2015, Bill Jack
All rights reserved.

No part of this book may be reproduced in any form without express permission of the copyright holder.

**Printed in the United States by Chapbook Press.**

For Jared

# ACKNOWLEDGEMENTS

To Debbie TenBrink who continues to devote countless hours to the task of editing the galleys and who, in her own right, is a marvelous writer and story teller. She is the quintessential "Comma Queen" and I don't know where I'd be in all of this without her guidance and her friendship.

To Chip Behler, a friend for almost a lifetime, who has been a cheerleader par excellence ever since I got this idea of writing fiction. Until now, he has been on the sidelines waving the pink hanky in support and encouragement but this time he volunteered to give me another set of eyes especially on some of the law related parts. His insights and intelligence and humor and the incredible time he has taken has made this story immensely better and more readable. But we'll never agree on commas.

To Rebecca Sitterly whose unwavering support has been so important in making sure the characters keep getting off the couch and whose cover art is without question the best part of the book.

Thank you

# CHAPTER ONE
## SHIT

"Shit!" Will's voice rang out and Dan Metz and Rusty Rhoades looked at each other and rolled their eyes. The word had been used on at least an hourly basis since Will Bennett a month ago had joined the two man crew roughing in a new house on White Lake on the west coast of Michigan. At first it had startled the two men into thinking something really serious had happened but, as time wore on, it was clear that it simply meant Will had screwed something else up. Dan's take was that they were losing time and money with Will on the job because usually one of them had to fix whatever Will had done wrong. Rusty's response was simple: Will was working for minimum wage so anything he did well was good for both of them. Still, even he had to agree that fixing Will's mistakes was a little tiresome. On the other hand, it was usually great comedy. As long as the new owner of the house never found the mistakes.

Rusty, the boss, had put in place several precautions from Day One. First, Will was not to operate any power tools that had blades; two, he was not to climb any ladders higher than a two step stool; and three, he was always to work on the job site where either Dan or Rusty had him in their sights. Unfortunately, this latest "shit" came when Will, on the second of the two steps and in clear view of Dan and Rusty, somehow managed to ricochet his hammer off some aluminum siding that wasn't even close to where he was hammering slamming it right back into his face. An examination of the results showed a small cut but fortunately nothing else. Rusty and Dan had quickly learned that the first aid kit had to be handy and Will's face was alcohol swabbed and Band Aided. Will looked at both of them knowing it was only a matter of time before one of them would either say something and start laughing or simply start laughing.  He wasn't wrong.  The act of somebody hitting himself in the face with his own hammer didn't require saying anything and it was some time before Dan and Rusty could bring themselves under control.  And even Will had to admit this was one of the better misadventures of his brief career as a fledgling carpenter.

Will had returned to Michigan six weeks before in a horrible funk.  He had taken a leave of absence from the Johnston & Blackwell firm on as short a notice as he could manage, passed his files off to other lawyers in the office, made sure Liz LaRue continued to have full employment with the firm, and ran for "home" with his proverbial tail between his legs.  The reason: his wife, the Honorable Alexandra Kennedy, had rekindled a relationship with a long ago lover who was also on the District Court bench where Alex served as the Chief Judge.  Will had heard the rumor from a drunk lawyer at the Coppertop one evening, had confronted Alex when he got home, and then had had to live with her answer.  There was a tearful explanation and the promise that the relationship, rekindled, had been short lived and the worst mistake she had ever made in her life.  But there it was.  Will heard little after Alex's affirmation  because of the roaring in his ears and the swelling in his throat.

That night he slept, or at least laid down, in the guest room, and the next morning packed some clothes and loaded them into his car.

He was the first person in the office and was making coffee when Morton Blackwell walked in.  By habit, they were almost always the first in and usually enjoyed some time together before the chaos of the day befell all of them.  Morton took one look at Will and was stunned.  Usually well-dressed even in business casual attire, Will was wrinkled from head to toe in clothes that may have been clean but certainly weren't ironed.  His eyes were bloodshot and his hair a mess.  He hadn't shaved, which was a first at least on a weekday.

"So. 'Sup?"  Stay calm, Morton, stay calm.

"Alex is having an affair with Don Jenkins." Flat with no affect.

The words sank in for a minute before Morton responded,

"Will, that rumor has been around for years, long before you ever appeared on the scene. Old news, my friend."

"Not so old. As in last night, not so old."

The two of them were quiet for a minute. In fact, Morton had heard that something between the two judges had gone on at the state judicial conference a month before but had dismissed it as old news recirculated and had kept it to himself. Alex and Will were as close as any two people could be and had survived murders, kidnappings, shootings and even the day to day agitations of life that drive relationships apart. As much as he loved his own wife, Morton had in a way envied Will and Alex their closeness.

Morton Blackwell had known Alex Kennedy for years, certainly before Will Bennett, and long before she had become a judge. She was one of the premier trial lawyers in the Southwest, if not the country, and had won several landmark cases in product liability, discrimination, and environmental torts, not to mention having earned some very healthy legal fees along the way. She had also earned a reputation as a "predatory cowgirl" who ran up boyfriends by the dozens, if the stories were to be believed, but had left them all behind as road kill. An exception had been Don Jenkins who had been appointed to the bench before Alex. Morton would see them together from time to time at bench-bar functions and had heard they were an item, but Morton was not one to pay attention to stuff like that. He knew there was a Mrs. Jenkins and some kids but little else.

Then Will Bennett had come along and things seemed to change. Alex was appointed to the District Court bench, quickly earned a reputation as a tough and fair-minded jurist, and then married this guy from Michigan. To others, she had never seemed happier or more content.

And now this.

"I got nothing going for a while this morning, Will. Breakfast someplace?"

"No thanks, Morton.  Got some thinking to do."

## CHAPTER TWO
## RUNNING FOR IT

Will poured his coffee, stuck his "In Conference" sign on the door of his office, went in and closed it tight. He needed to be alone. From the time he had met her, Alex Kennedy had been the love of his life. They had had terrible times, ridiculous arguments, pulled the trigger on the relationship time and again, and had somehow survived. Married now for almost four years, they had surprised their closest friends by staying together. Will had left his practice in Michigan and had moved to New Mexico to practice law. He had never been happier. His daughter, Grace, was back in Michigan but they texted or talked daily and she was making her own life in her hometown.

And now this.

Will found his anti-anxiety pills in the top drawer of his desk and swallowed two. He realized he was hyperventilating and that a major headache was just around the corner and coming on fast. He was paralyzed. Truly paralyzed. He had heard about people's worlds crashing down around them but, even in the worst of times, he had never felt this kind of devastation. He thought about suicide and homicide and ruled out homicide. Suicide he left on the table. After all, he had had a good life, he'd earned a good living, made some friends, and had a wonderful, loving, talented daughter. Until last night, he thought he'd had a great marriage. But if the future was more of the same, only without Alex, what was the point of that? Waiting for some doctor to tell him he had cancer? Having a heart attack in the midst of a closing argument? Why not get out now?

As the minutes wore on, he knew he couldn't stay in New Mexico. He had moved to Albuquerque only because of Alex, had convinced his longtime assistant, Liz LaRue, to move as well and now here he was without the anchor he always thought he'd have.

He reflected on the past months searching for any signs of discontent but he simply hadn't seen any at all.  If anything, he thought he and Alex were closer than ever, especially after she had been kidnapped by a madman and then rescued.  So why now?  For some reason, he wasn't even angry.  Just devastated.  Years ago, Alex had told him about Don Jenkins, but he had discarded it as part of the past and had never given it a second thought.  God knew he had his own past.

The pills kicked in, he calmed a bit, and thought to look at his trial calendar.  Other than a medical malpractice case two months down the road, there was nothing.  Or at least nothing that couldn't be handled by his partners in the firm.  Plus, settlement overtures on the part of the defense had already occurred.  It was a very good case, so he guessed that it would settle at some point, probably after the defense lawyer had billed enough hours to justify his existence.  So there was a calm that could get him out of New Mexico and away from Alex for good.

That's what he needed.  To get away from Alex Kennedy for good.


Will took one more deep breath and began to formulate a plan.  He would move back to Michigan because that was the only place he knew other than New Mexico.  He still had his lake house.  He could move in there, at least for the next six months until winter set in.  He would be closer to Grace and that would be good.  Alex and Will had kept their finances pretty much separate since they had married and he mentally added up how much he had in his savings and retirement accounts.  Probably not as much as he should at his age but enough to get him by for a while.  He wondered idly if his old firm would take him back.  He had left on reasonably good terms and thought it likely it would, but he really wasn't sure at the moment whether practicing law was really something he wanted to do any more.

Right now alcoholism sounded like a pretty good career track.

# CHAPTER THREE
## IN CHAMBERS

Alex Kennedy sat in her chambers after her own sleepless night and tried to make sense of what she had done to herself and to the man she loved like no other. There was no way to make any sense of it. She had screwed up the one thing that she thought was inviolate, the one relationship after all the others that had been consistent and loving and challenging and pure. In one incredibly stupid weekend, she had thrown it all away.

She had missed the last several annual judicial conferences in large part because she didn't want to face Don Jenkins or have anything to do with him. Once she became chief judge of the biggest court in New Mexico, and the conference became more difficult to avoid, she had gone. At the Friday night cocktail party in Santa Fe, Jenkins had approached her and wouldn't leave her alone, asking about her life, telling her about his (his wife who after all these years still didn't understand him), his kids now grown, still on the bench but counting down the days to retirement, how great she looked, how he missed all the wonderful times they had had together. On and on and on. He sat next to her at dinner and continued the onslaught. Maybe it was the wine, maybe it was the compliments, and maybe it was the memories of old times. There had certainly been some good ones in the years they had known each other. And they ended up in bed together.

The sex wasn't any better than it had ever been and after it was over, all Alex could think of was Will and what she had done to him. She asked Jenkins to leave her room, but he wanted to stay, and she let him. The next morning he left early, enough so that she hoped no one would notice.

But the damage was done. Too many of the judges were aware of their past relationship and too many of them had seen them having dinner together and drinks afterward. She should have known better and had nobody to blame but herself.

The next morning Jenkins approached her at breakfast talking about what a great night it had been and wouldn't it be great to put the band back together after all these years.  Alex had thrown up as soon as he had left her hotel room, she was now drinking water, the thought of coffee on her stomach more than she could take.  She spent the rest of the day avoiding him  until Saturday night when they met at the bar.  She asked him outside to the patio, explained that getting together was a terrible mistake, telling him she was, for the first time, happily in a long term relationship, and that their relationship was over for good.  That might have worked save for the kiss on the cheek that too many people saw through the windows out to the patio.

Rumors began as soon as the Monday after the conference.  That afternoon, Karen Stillson, Alex's best friend and case manager, walked into Alex's chambers without knocking, shut the door behind her, sat down and said, "What the fuck did you do with Don Jenkins in Santa Fe?"

And that's when Alex knew it was only a matter of time before the rumors got back to Will.  The Albuquerque bar was too small and too incestuous to let a rumor go by like the chief judge of Bernalillo County getting involved again with her longtime lover. In some ways, she wondered why it had taken as long as it did for Will to find out.  But find out he did, and here she was.

She had been surprised and shaken by how calm Will had been when he confronted her and when she told him what had happened.  What she didn't and couldn't know was how little he had heard after she told him it was true.  When she was done he had turned around and gone upstairs to the guest bedroom.  She briefly heard him the next morning but he didn't bother with a shower.  He simply left.

Alex considered her options and agonized over what she had done.  She knew she would survive.  Hell, judges in Bernalillo County had done far worse and kept their jobs.  This wasn't even worthy enough to attract media attention.  But for Alex Kennedy, it couldn't have been worse because it wasn't about her job or even her reputation.  It was about single handedly losing what mattered most to her.  She thought about calling or emailing Will but there was really nothing to say.  Hey, Will, I screwed an old lover a few weeks ago but it didn't mean anything and I still love you and what's for dinner?  Not likely.  She knew him and his pride too well.

Karen Stillson knocked (this time) and came in and delivered the daily schedule.  She had been cool to Alex ever since that Monday after the conference and Alex couldn't blame her.

After Karen left, the phone rang.  She recognized the number from Don Jenkins' chambers.  She let it ring to voice mail, put her head on her desk, and began to cry.

# CHAPTER FOUR
# HOMEWARD BOUND

By midmorning Will had put his plan together.  He had to leave New Mexico right away.  He called Liz LaRue, Morton Caldwell, and Jackie LaPointe into his office at 11 AM.  Neither Jackie nor Liz knew anything about the rumors and were incredulous when Will announced he was taking a leave of absence from the firm for an unspecified period of time for personal reasons.  They each asked questions, the answers to which they deserved, but he said nothing other than he needed to get away.  Morton remained silent.

The four of them went over the files and the decision was made to reassign almost all of them to Rosalind McManus.  She had come from Legal Services and in the short time she had been with the firm had already established herself as the next bright young litigation star.  She would embrace the challenge and would prosper with the new responsibility.  Jackie was in her third year at UNM Law School and had already accepted a position with the firm after she graduated.  She would second chair Rosalind.  Liz would stay with the firm unless she wanted to go elsewhere, but Morton assured her that her job with the firm was secure and important.  She was crying uncontrollably.

When they were done, Will asked to have a few minutes alone with Liz.  While he wasn't specific, he told her that he and Alex were having some struggles and that it was best for him to leave Albuquerque for a while.

"You ever comin' back?"

He looked at her for a long time.  They had been through so much and he felt guilty as hell about leaving her behind.  On the other hand, she had found a new life in New Mexico and had never been happier.  She would be OK.  Always had been, always would be.

"I'm not sure.  I doubt it."

Liz nodded and stood to leave.

"Whatever the demons, boss man, I hope you beat them."

"Love you, Liz."

"Love you, Will."

At noon, he drove to the townhouse in Old Town that he shared with Alex.  He packed a few things: a couple of suits and ties if he ever decided to practice law or, if he didn't, to go to funerals; his favorite weekend boots; his favorite jeans.  He thought about taking the mountain bike but left it.  He had one in Michigan that worked fine.  Within an hour he was done.

Will took a last look around the place.  It had been so much a part of him that it felt like he was leaving part of his physical self.  He hugged Jinks and Josie, the two black cats who owned the place, and knew he would miss them both.  He considered writing a note to Alex but really could not think of a single thing to say that would help the pain.

He needed to be gone.

Will stopped at the credit union on the way back to the office and emptied the savings account that was in both their names but was only his money.  He took his name off Alex's account.  His retirement fund back in Michigan had never been changed over so that would stay.  He closed his checking account and took it all in cash. He hoped to hell he didn't get robbed on the way to Michigan.


Back at the office, Jackie, Liz, and Will put the final plans together.  It was surprisingly simple especially because they hadn't told Rosalind what was happening.  By day's end, Will had taken what he needed from his office and was ready to go.

He loved Liz and Jackie and promised he would stay in touch.  He hoped they would visit him in Michigan and both said they would.  He kept the firm email and voice mail and would check it routinely, and they had his cell phone.  Then there was nothing else to say.

"I'm sorry to do this, you guys, but I have to. Someday you'll understand. Or not. Morton will announce the leave of absence tomorrow morning at a staff meeting."

Each in turn, in tears, hugged him and he, in tears, hugged them back.

Will Bennett walked out of the office, got in the Subaru, and headed east.

## CHAPTER FIVE
## ALONE

Alex sleepwalked through the rest of the day as she dealt with the mundane machinations of the wheels of justice. She walked into the townhouse with a sense of dread and knew, without even looking, that Will had left. It was too empty of spirit and soul, and even Josie and Jinks were out of sorts, keeping their distance as though they knew it was all her fault. She checked closets and dresser drawers and saw that some but not all of Will's things were missing. He had left her and she didn't blame him.

She poured herself a Jameson's and thought about life without Will. She was a survivor. She would survive this but she'd never get over it. It had been too good, they had been through too much, and now it was done. Alex felt a sudden burst of anger at Will for leaving her just because of a meaningless tryst with somebody from long ago after too much wine had been consumed. But that wasn't fair and she knew it.

She poured herself another Jameson's and then, on a whim, called Robert Davison back in Virginia. Robert had been the detective who had investigated the murder of Will's friend's wife, and who had saved Will's life at the end. Will and Robert had become great friends and, at one point, there had even been an attraction between Alex and Robert that fortunately had never been consummated. Jesus, Alex, you are such a whore. Robert had married Alicia Dawe, the chief of detectives, and they had just recently had their first child. Robert was a private investigator now and Alicia was still rising in the ranks of the Alexandria Police Department.

She got him on his cell, made sure he had the time to talk, took a deep breath, and told him the whole story ending with Will packing up and leaving for parts unknown. Robert listened in silence. When she was done, he said:

"How do you want it to end, Alex? How should the story end?"

"I love him, Robert, and I always will.  I want him back.  I need him back."

"Given what you've told me, how could he ever get back to Albuquerque?"

Silence for a minute.  "I don't know.  I'm not sure he could or would.  Or even should."

Again silence.  "I'm not sure either.  You think he's going to Michigan?"

"Probably.  Grace is there, Rusty is there, the lake house is there, the old firm is there if they'll take him back.  I don't know where else he'd go."

"OK, I'm going to give it a couple of days.  If he's going to Michigan, he'll be in a hurry and he'll get there by then and I'll call him.  What do you want me to tell him, Alex?"

Again silence.  "Whatever it takes to get him to come back to me, Robert."

"Might have thought about that a little bit ago," he said softly.

"I know, Robert, I know."

"Goodbye, Alex, I'll do what I can."

"I know you will.  Goodbye, Robert, thank you.  Love to Alicia."

Robert clicked off and shook his head.

Humans.  It's a wonder we've lasted as long as we have.

CHAPTER SIX
THE JOURNEY

Will got four hours out of Albuquerque and crashed.  The lack of sleep the night before and the emotional wreckage of his life was overwhelming.  The second or third time he drove off the road he found a rest area, pulled in as close to the facilities as he could, locked the doors, and put the seat back.  He was asleep within minutes.

He had spent the trip going over in his mind his life with Alex, almost like it was a movie, from the time they had met to the times they had gotten to know each other and finally  to the time they had made the decision to marry and settle in New Mexico.  Interspersed between the montages of that life were visions of Alex in bed with Don Jenkins and it was those scenes that kept him driving as long as he did.  They would keep coming back to him over and over no matter what he did to try to change the channel.  In his head, he knew it would get better.  Just not now.

Four or five hours later, he woke up and, for the longest time, had no idea where he was.  Mercifully it had been a sleep without dreams or nightmares and, thankfully, nobody had robbed or killed him.  When Will finally gathered his wits and realized he was in his car in a rest area in eastern New Mexico, alone in the universe, it was almost a relief.  He found his Dopp kit and stumbled into the facility to pull himself together.  No shave but a quick face wash and tooth brushing and he was back in the car and ready to go.  It was still dark outside, but it was spring and the days were getting longer and he could make out the beginnings of the day as he got back on I-40 and headed east again.  As the dawn brightened, the desert came alive with its hues of reds and greens and browns.  Will had come to love the desert in the time he had spent in the Southwest and marveled at the vast array of sights and smells and sounds.  He wondered if he would ever see it again.

Stopping only for gas and fast food, he drove straight through to Michigan.  For a good part of the trip, he revisited the movie of his life with Alex.  As the miles went by, he was able to clear his mind of the images of her with another man and concentrate on the good things they had had.  And there had been many.  Which made this whole thing so awful.  By the time he hit Missouri, he began to think about the future.  He wondered if he had been too hasty in leaving New Mexico but discarded that thought almost immediately.  Given the circumstances, he couldn't see himself staying in the same town with Alex, knowing that every time he walked into a courtroom or a restaurant or a bar he would wonder who knew what.  Maybe after some time had passed he would be able to do that, but not now, and likely not for a long time.

So then what?  It was a weird feeling of complete disconnection driving in the middle of the United States.  Not a soul knew where he was, not Alex, not Grace, not his friends or law partners.  Nobody.  Will could not remember a time when that had happened and it gave him a sense of both loss and freedom, of despair and empowerment all at the same time.  He wondered what the future held for him, especially now in his mid-fifties.  Life had all been mapped out at least for the immediate future and now it wasn't and he was on his way back to Michigan to uncertainty upon uncertainty.

The immediate plan of course was to go to the lake house because being there would most center him.  Rusty had gotten the place open a few weeks before and the water was turned on so it was good to go.  It was mid-May, a beautiful time in Michigan…unless it was snowing.  So he would go there, get the place stocked up, and then take stock of himself.

The problem was that all he had ever done was practice law and he had no other skill set that could earn him even the barest of livelihoods.  He had often thought about working in a hardware store or a bookstore or a library and the small towns near the lake house had all of those things.  He thought again about contacting his old firm to see if they would take him back.  He had kept his Michigan license to practice law current so that wasn't a problem, but maybe the larger issue was whether he wanted to continue to try cases and whether the firm would want him.  He had kept in touch with some of his peers and the firm was prospering.  Why would they want to bring in somebody his age?  With no clients of his own at least for the immediate future, he was just another mouth to feed.

He was without an anchor.  Alex had been that for him and now she wasn't.  Somewhere in southern Illinois, the thought crossed his mind that maybe after some time had passed they could somehow put their relationship back together.  At least a friendship.  That gave him some comfort but the thought of her with Judge Jenkins or even somebody else was more than he could get his mind around, so he pushed on.


Tired to the bone, he arrived at the lake house around 4 AM, turned the heat on,  and fell into bed, only to wake up three hours later with Rusty Rhoades sitting next to his bed in a chair with a shotgun across his lap staring at him.

"What the…?!?"

" 'What the' is right.  What the hell are you doing here?"

"This is my house, asshole.  What are you doing in it with a gun in your lap?"

Rusty put the gun down on the floor.

"I was out for my walk and saw fresh tracks leading into your place.  Saw a car and thought somebody had broken in so I went back and got my shotgun.  You forgot to lock the door."

Will got out of bed.  He'd never even taken his clothes off.

"Coffee?"  Will assumed there was some in the pantry.

"Sure.  What the hell are you doing here, Will?"

"You just asked me that.  It's kind of a long story.  Let me get the coffee going and I'll fill you in."

So he did.  He left nothing out.

The two of them drained the pot of coffee.  Rusty was uncharacteristically quiet while Will spoke.  When he was done Rusty simply said, "Wow."

“No shit.”

“What are you gonna do?”

“No idea.  Take a few days and settle in here.  Bug the crap out of you and your lovely   Reba Sue.  Take some time for myself.”

“You talk to Alex?”

“Not since she told me.  Not much to talk about.”

Rusty was quiet for a time.

“You two have something special, you know.”

“Yup.  That’s what makes it so hard.”

“Yup.  Put your boots on.  Let’s get a walk in.”

Even though he’d only had three hours’ sleep in the last twenty four, Will pulled on his favorite boots and off they went walking through the pine woods behind the lake house.  They were quiet most of the way, enjoying each other’s company and the beauty of the morning.  Michigan was full blown into spring with the dragonfly-new-green leaves on the trees and a cool freshness filling the air.  The trillium were in full bloom and the two men stopped from time to time for possible Morel sightings.

When they got back, Rusty said he was off to work.  He was building a new house on White Lake and was still roughing it in.  Long hours but wanting to finish that part of it so they could get inside.  He told Will he’d stop by at the end of the day.

“I am so sorry, man.”

“Thanks, dude.  I guess it’ll all work out.”

“Maybe you should call her and let her know where you are.”

“Maybe.”

Rusty left and Will looked around the place at all the old familiar pieces of his past.  Sam Greenberg was here, Will’s best friend who had spent many wonderful times at the lake house and who had died here.  Grace was here, and of course Alex.  It felt like home.

## CHAPTER SEVEN
## GETTING SETTLED

Too wide awake to go back to bed, Will showered and found the clothes that he always left at the house. He drove to the grocery store in town, stocked up on the basics, and put everything away when he got back home.

He checked the time and it was noon. He hooked up his computer, got a signal, and emailed Liz to tell her he had made it back to Michigan and was at the lake house. Almost immediately he heard back from her. Everyone in the firm had been in shock when Morton Blackwell had called them together to tell them about Will's leave of absence. Lots of questions that Morton had ducked simply saying that Will's privacy was to be respected and that when he knew more he would let people know. Liz and Jackie had started to get Rosalind McManus up to speed on the cases and they were letting his clients know. Will felt badly about leaving everybody in the lurch, especially the clients, but really felt he had no choice. He had simply had to get away. So far everything seemed to be going smoothly and Will wondered why anybody ever thought they were indispensable. Because nobody ever is.

He replied that everything sounded good and he would be in touch. Got a "love you" back from Liz and that was it.

His cell phone rang and he recognized the number. He thought about not answering but that didn't seem quite right so he did.

"Alex."

"It's Karen, Will. Let me get her."

"Will?"

"Alex."

"Where are you?"

"Lake house."

"You OK?"

"Sure. You?"

"Sure." Silence.

"I'm glad you're there, Will."

"Me too."

"When are you coming back?"

What a weird ass question that is, he thought to himself.

"Not sure, Alex. I took a leave of absence from the firm."

"God, I am so sorry, Will."

"Me too."

"Will you stay in touch?"

"Sure."

"OK then. I'm glad you're safe."

"Thanks. Thanks for calling." Geez, really Will?

I miss you so much, Will, she thought. But the connection was over.

God, I miss us, he thought. But the connection was over.

Will took a deep breath and thought about what to do next. He busied himself with getting the place cleaned, windows washed, carpets vacuumed, dead ladybugs wiped up. He remembered how much Grace used to love ladybugs.

Grace. Damn. He hadn't told her anything about any of this and hadn't communicated in over three days. He texted her that he was at the lake house and got an instant reply that she was in court and would call him back on a break.

Grace had stayed on with a federal judge as a semi-permanent clerk in Grand Rapids. Some months ago she had been the victim of a vicious assault that had left her in a coma for several days. She had recovered, at least physically, and with the judge's permission had extended her clerkship for at least another year. Forty five minutes later his cell phone rang.

"Dad! You all right?"

"Of course, honey. How 'bout you?"

"Yeah, I'm fine. Why are you at the lake house? What's going on?"

Will thought for a minute before answering.

"Thought I'd take some time off to regroup and think about what I want to do with the rest of my life. It's good to be here."

"Alex with you?"

He thought for another minute. Alex and Grace had had a bumpy start in their own relationship, but as time went on they had liked each other more and more and now were good friends. Will was pretty sure Grace didn't need to know that part of the story.

"Nope. Too much going on with the wheels of justice back in New Mexico. So it's just me."

"How long will you be here?"

"Not sure about that. A while. Can we get together for dinner or lunch? I'll come to GR."

"God, yes. How 'bout tomorrow night?"

"Perfect. Pick you up at your new apartment?" Grace had moved out of the apartment where the attack had taken place and had found a new, smaller one still in the historic downtown district. She had sent pictures and it looked wonderful.

"Perfect. Six?"

"Excellent. See you then. Love you, Grace."

"Love you, Dad."

He hung up and felt the best he had in days. Even when she had been a little girl, Grace had always been his center and now more than ever.

That afternoon Will took a long walk on the beach. It was a beautiful, sunny day with a spring breeze coming out of the southwest. He walked into it on the way out, got three or four miles to the south and then turned around. The water was its various shades of blue from dark navy farther out to the different shades of turquoise in closer where the sand bars ran along the coast. He tried to think of nothing but the present moment and that worked for a while, but then his thoughts would turn back to Alex. Always to Alex. He wondered what she was doing at that very moment and tried to guess. Maybe on the bench or maybe in chambers. It occurred to him that they had been so busy with their respective careers, Alex as chief judge and Will with his new firm, that they had forgotten to pay enough attention to each other. Perhaps that had caused her to cross over.  He hadn't given that a thought until just now.  Maybe that was the problem - he hadn't given it a thought.  Too late now.  He trudged the rest of the way home.

Rusty stopped by after work and had a beer.

"I have a great idea, Will.  Why don't you join Dan Metz and me and help us build the house?  We're at that stage where more hands can really be helpful.  We're working on the shore of White Lake, and its springtime."

Will thought about it for a minute and began to make excuses like no tools of his own to speak of, like no skills to speak of, like he'd been sitting on his ass for weeks at a time without exercise.

Rusty would have none of it.

"I got all the tools you'll need.  I'm not asking for a master carpenter, I'm asking for a grunt, and it will do you good to get off your ass.  It's Thursday.  You'll start Monday.  I'll pick you up at 7 sharp.

And so the shit began.

The next night Will drove into Grand Rapids and picked his daughter up at her apartment.  It was a one bedroom, one bath affair on the second floor of a beautiful old brick Victorian house decorated with an eclectic mix of old and new that suited Grace to a T.  He took her to one of his old haunts that still had the best fish, fresh water or ocean, in Michigan and caught her up on things with Alex.  He didn't tell her about the affair with Jenkins and left it that they were struggling and he had wanted to get away.  She listened carefully and when he was done, she said quietly, "Alex called me today.  I know all about what happened."

"Shit happens.  What happened to you last year shouldn't have and what happened to Alex and me shouldn't have.  But they did."

"She still loves you, Dad."

He thought about that for a moment.

"Then why?"

"She doesn't know why.  She only knows she loves you."

They decided to change the subject and the rest of the dinner was taken up with Grace filling her dad in on her life, her job, her friends.  She had had a couple of dates with an architect she had met at a party and that seemed to make her happy, but she was quick to point out that it would be a long time before anything serious came of it.  He told her about Rusty offering him a job and that stopped her in her tracks.

"Dad, you can't change a light bulb."

"I know, I'm a little worried.   But it will be good to be outside and maybe I can learn something."

"God, be careful, OK?  He's not going to let you use power tools, is he?"

"I'll pass along your concerns."

At the end of the evening, they made plans to have brunch at the lake house on Sunday.

He dropped her at her apartment and she gave him a long hug.

"She still loves you, Dad.  Please don't give up."

On the way back to the lake house, he wondered about that.

"All rise."

Lawyers, prisoners, family members of the prisoners, and court staff all rose as the Honorable Alexandra Kennedy entered the courtroom. It was Zoo Day at the Bernalillo County Courthouse when several dozen prisoners were paraded before her to plead not guilty to various and sundry charges ranging from robbery to rape to murder to domestic violence and all felony points in between. Those who were fortunate enough to be represented had their counsel present. Those not so fortunate were appointed lawyers either from the overworked corps of public defenders or from the list of contract lawyers the county had set up to handle the overflow. The paperwork on each was handled by her court staff and Judge Kennedy had the luxury of letting her mind wander.

In days past, she would sadly marvel at the human carnage that was paraded before her, but today she almost enjoyed the mundaneness of it all just so she didn't have to keep thinking of what a mess her life was in.

Word of Will's leave of absence had reverberated throughout the Albuquerque bar and word that it had stemmed from Alex and Will getting separated had only added fuel to the fire of gossip. What role her night with Don Jenkins played in Will's departure and how many people knew about the night, she had no idea. Jenkins had called her on several occasions since the judicial conference and she had been polite but firm that there would be no reprise, not from years ago and not from a month ago. He persisted and she finally, abruptly, rudely told him to go fuck himself. It would make for some difficult judges' meetings that she had to preside over as chief judge but it was what it was going to be.

Friends had rallied for her.  Karen Stillson had gotten over her initial shock and Margaret Espinoza, the Albuquerque detective who had become a close friend, had also been there for her.  Trouble was her friends all loved Will Bennett and so 'he had it coming' or 'he deserved it, the son of a bitch' was never a part of the conversation.  She had called Grace who had brought her up to date on what Will was doing.

"He's working with Rusty?  Is he crazy?  He'll kill himself!"

Grace assured her that Rusty would keep him away from anything dangerous and, in fact, Grace had called Rusty to remind him of that.  By that time, 'shit' had already become a major part of the day for Dan and Rusty so it wasn't like Grace was telling him anything he didn't already know.

Robert Davison had also called Alex.  He had spoken with Will at length on a couple of occasions.  Will was hurting but trying to be stoic.

"He still loves you, Alex.  I know that for sure.  I'm just not clear on how, or if, you all can put it back together.  You hurt him pretty good."

"I know, Robert, I know."

"Not to worry.  I'll keep talking to him, and we're planning on getting out to Michigan the end of June so that will give us a good chance to walk the beach and talk it out."

"You think I should go to Michigan?"

"No, not yet.  Let some more time pass."

And so more time did pass and with it came a sense of normalcy to most of the participants in the drama.  Will kept showing up on the job site and kept yelling 'shit' on a regular basis.  Even Dan Metz got used to it.  As near as Rusty could tell, there wasn't a fingernail on either of Will's hands that wasn't in danger of falling off at some point due to self-inflicted injuries from one trauma or another.  On the other hand, both Rusty and

Dan noticed that Will was handling himself with more confidence and maybe even the 'shits' were getting a little more spaced out.

Grace saw her dad at least once a week and they communicated daily.  Will even suggested she invite her architect friend out to the lake for a picnic but Grace wasn't there yet.  Except when he was working, Will kept to himself, and Rusty and Reba Sue respected that.  Each day after work Will would strip down and go swimming in Lake Michigan.  The lake in early June is not known for its warmth but that didn't matter.  But for the fingernails, Will was in better shape than he had been in years.

In Albuquerque, Judge Kennedy had the day to day work of the court to keep her mind off Will.  She relished presiding over trials, especially with good trial lawyers, and that carried her from one day to the next.  Like Will, she kept to herself for the most part, save for the occasional dinner with Margaret or Karen.  She started working out again at the gym and was toning up and losing some unwanted pounds.

But beneath the surface, Alex and Will were miserable.  A dozen times a day one of them would see something in life and want nothing more than to share it with the other.  At least a dozen times a day one would want to call the other just to hear the other's voice.  But they couldn't and wouldn't, and wondered if they ever would again.

Emissaries stayed in touch throughout.  Grace contacted Alex at least once a week as did Robert.  Karen, Jackie, and Liz also communicated with both of them just to make sure connections were not completely broken.

On a Saturday in the third week of June, Will was at the lake house fixing his boat up and getting ready for an afternoon of fishing.  To him, fishing and catching fish were two different sports.  He had gotten very good at fishing but catching fish was an

art he hadn't yet mastered.  There was a knock at the door and
Robert Davison was standing there.  Will looked behind him for
Alicia, Robert's kids, the new arrival - but there was nobody.

"Mind if I come in?"

Will stood to the side and Robert walked in.

"Direct flights from National to Grand Rapids are the
bomb, man.  Nothing to it.  Beautiful day.  Let's walk the beach.
I've only got a couple of hours and then I've got to head back."

Will put aside the thought of fishing and still in a state of
shock walked down to the beach beside his friend.

"A little over a year ago, you and I talked and I told you
Alicia and I were having some problems.  Stresses at work, the
interracial marriage thing, and too many kids with too many
problems.  'Member?"

"Yup."

"That wasn't quite the whole story.  Shortly after I started
the PI gig, one of my first clients and I had a very short fling.
Alicia found out and, as you can imagine 'cause you know her, she
was homicidal.  I mean seriously homicidal.  But you know what?
We talked and talked and talked and I realized how much I loved
her and how stupid it was and how much I wanted to be with her
and work it out.  You know what she said?"

"Nope."

"You ever ever go looking for strange again and you are
going to be in the market for some serious organs 'cause you're
gonna be missin' some.  You remember what you told me, don't
you?"

"Not really."

"You told me to do everything I could to make it work
because good relationships were worth working for.  Then you told
me to get my ass and Alicia's ass out to here."  Robert waved at
the lake.

"And we did.  And we found ourselves again.  And we've
got little Wendy to show for it.  It was 'cause of you, Will, and
'cause Alicia found it in her heart to forgive me.  And we've never

been better. And now you need to start thinking and believing and living what you told me."

They walked in silence for a good while and then turned back towards the house so Robert could get back on a plane and get home to his loved ones.

"You need to think about what I said and you need to do the right thing, Will. She has never stopped loving you. She did a really stupid thing and she hates herself for it, but you know what, man? It's body parts pure and simple. And don't tell me you haven't at least been tempted since the two of you have been together. Only difference? You weren't drunk enough to act on it. And you know it. And you know I know it. Don't fuck this up."

They hugged for a long time and then Robert was back in his rental car heading to Grand Rapids leaving Will in the wake of a friendship he wasn't sure he could ever have had again after Sam Greenberg's death at the lake house so many months ago. After Sam died and after all that had gone on tracking his murderer including Will's own near death, Will had felt a huge emptiness but he had Rusty and he had Robert and they helped fill the void.

That night Will drank three quarters of a fifth of Jameson Irish whiskey and fell asleep on the deck chair. He was still there the next morning when Rusty stopped by to see if he wanted to take a walk. He didn't. But for Rusty helping him out of the deck chair, he might still be there.

That day, after several Tylenol, he got the boat out, hooked it to the Subaru, and drove to Blue Lake. It was his favorite lake not because he ever caught any fish there but because the launch was so big even he could get his boat in the water. It was still early enough in the season that he practically had the lake to himself. He found his favorite spot, baited up, and got to thinking.

Robert was right, of course, about most of what he had said. Will had been tempted but the difference wasn't alcohol. It was that he had found in Alex his one true sexual partner and after all the starts and stops in his life, he hadn't wanted to risk this one true thing.  But Alex had followed through and that was a big difference.  On the other hand, it really was just body parts and why should one stupid transgression destroy everything the two of them had built?  Whoa.  Will was so deep in thought he almost missed a bite and, much to his surprise, hauled in a lovely fat bluegill.  For the next hour, he forgot his troubles and was suddenly catching bluegills – big ones – every time he threw a line in.  He looked around hoping somebody would see his success and then thought better of it.  No sense giving away his favorite spot.  When he got to twenty keepers, he quit.  There was only him to feed, so why get greedy.

Then crowding in was how much Alex loved blue gills. Arg.

## CHAPTER NINE
### WE NEED YOU

For the next several days, Will thought about nothing but Alex. He tried to stay in the moment, especially at work. Rusty had actually let him use a staple gun for the first time and the last thing he wanted to do was shoot himself or anybody else for that matter. He was not so oblivious to fail to notice that whenever he picked up the gun both Dan and Rusty, while still in eyesight of him, were not in shooting range.

At night he would envision calling Alex, get to the part where he said 'hello,' and then never get any farther. Jesus, she was his wife, they knew each other better than anybody, and he was acting like the asshole he had been most of his adolescent and adult life. Must be all his mother's fault. Then he would find some reason not to call, like it was all Alex's fault, so why should he call her? So of course nothing happened.

What he didn't know was that Alex was back in Albuquerque having those exact same thoughts. What would she say after 'hello?' 'What's new?' 'How 'bout them Tigers?' She knew Will so well that she knew she would have to be the one to make a move if a move was to be made. She knew herself well enough to know that it would be next to impossible for her to do that. So of course nothing happened.


That Friday at the job site, Dan, Rusty, and Will were eating lunch and talking about how much progress they had made. The exterior framing of the house was about 90% completed and they were getting ready to tackle the inside.

A nondescript car pulled into the driveway and stopped, the door opened, and Morton Blackwell climbed out.

It took Will a moment to make the connection and then he walked over, shook Morton's hand, and gave him a hug. Rusty and Dan stayed back, not sure what to make of this stranger, but Will introduced them all and explained who Morton was. Will had talked about his law cases from time to time but Rusty did not know any of his partners.  Rusty felt a foreboding about why Morton Blackwell would travel all the way from Albuquerque to see Will.  Why the hell wouldn't he just pick up the phone and call him?

Morton waited a moment to give Rusty and Dan the chance to give him some space with Will.  They never moved, just stood there like body guards, and Morton thought to himself, what the hell.  If Will doesn't care, I don't care.

"We need you.  We need you back, Will."

Will just stared at him.  In the weeks that he had been away, the thought of practicing law again had rarely crossed his mind.  He had not contacted his old firm and had never given a single thought to returning to either Albuquerque or to Johnston & Blackwell.

"What's up, Morton?"

"You remember the Ruiz case?"

"Vaguely."  It had been one of his partner Luis's cases.  He recalled that Luis was trying to prove willful and intentional misconduct on the part of Mr. Ruiz's employer, attempting to get around the workers' compensation ban against suing your own employer if you were hurt at work.  A New Mexico Supreme Court case named after a man named Junior Delgado held that, in very special circumstances where the conduct of the employer was so egregious, an employee could sue his own boss.  Even in a state as liberal as New Mexico, it was very difficult to survive a motion to dismiss by the employer.  Will recalled that Mr. Ruiz was a bit of a miscreant by all accounts who had been killed in a cave in at his job with a local excavation company.

"We survived the motion to dismiss.  The judge denied any emergency appeal.  He set the trial for a month from next Monday."

"That's great, Morton.  Tell Luis I wish him well."

"That's why I'm here, Will. Two days ago, Luis had a heart attack. He's alive and resting but is scheduled for a bypass next week. He's out of commission for the foreseeable future."

"So the judge will adjourn the trial, right?"

"No. I had a conference with the court and defense counsel yesterday. The lawyer objected and the judge agreed we had enough horses and enough time to get ready. He denied our motion to adjourn."

"What asshole lawyer would do something like object when the other side's lawyer had a heart attack?"

"Roy McDaniels."

Of all of the lawyers Will had met in Albuquerque, hell anywhere, few were as big a prick as Roy McDaniels. Genuinely reviled by the plaintiff's bar and, truth be known, by the defense bar as well, McDaniels was the quintessential take no prisoners defense lawyer. He never agreed to anything, never compromised on anything, and tried almost everything…even when in most people's eyes it was in his client's best interests not to go to trial. He had won a lot of big cases but had lost a lot of big ones as well, often forcing his clients into bankruptcy after an adverse verdict.

"You're here because you want me to come back and try the case for the Ruiz family?"

"That's why I'm here, Will."

Rusty, who had overheard every word, now understood why Morton Blackwell had flown all the way to Michigan to meet with Will. He would have done the same thing.

There was a silence as Will weighed his options. He hadn't for a minute missed the trial work and the stress of litigation. He had hated being away from Alex and Albuquerque but that had been his choice. He had found a life back in Michigan that had suited him for the short term. The thought of going back and living in the same city as his wife, of doing battle against one of the real jerks of the profession, of working 18 hours a day from now through trial all seemed so daunting.

He looked at Rusty and Dan.  "What do you guys think?"

Oddly, it was Dan who spoke first.

"Will, if it was me, I'd stay here doin' what I'm doin', workin' hard, drinkin' hard, fishin' and huntin' and livin' the good easy life among the people who care for me.  But it's you, and if I were you, I'd go back to Albuquerque, face the demons, and try the fuckin' case.  It's who you are."

Will looked at Rusty who nodded in agreement.

"Where are you staying, Morton?"

"Ramada back in town."

"Let me think about it tonight and we'll have breakfast in the morning.  You have a flight back tomorrow?"

"Leaves at one."

"You'll make it."

Morton shook hands with Rusty, Dan, and Will, got back in the rental and drove off.

Will looked at both men.  "Really?"

They both nodded.

"I'm that bad at this?" Waving his hand at the structure behind him.

"You're not THAT bad, Will, and you've really improved since you've been here."

Dan cut in, "But for a carpenter, you make a pretty good lawyer."

"You firing me?" Will looked at Rusty.

"Let's call it a leave of absence."

That night, for the first time in a long time, Will thought about what he wanted to do with the rest of his life.  Truth be told, he had always had an uneasy truce with being a trial lawyer.  He had loved the competition and loved being in trial, but the day to day stress of discovery, written questions to be answered, statements under oath to be taken, experts to be retained, jerks on the other side to deal with, all in the lead up to trial had taken their toll.

Other than the thoughts of Alex and their breakup that continued to cloud his mind, Will had so enjoyed being back in Michigan, working in the outdoors, spending time with Grace, and walking the beach of Lake Michigan.  He could see himself living a life like this and, if he were careful with his money and could find some nominal work, he could make a go of it.

His mind went back to the days of Johnston & Blackwell.  Relative strangers, the founding members of the firm had formed a bond like no other, especially after a number of the firm's lawyers were murdered by its office manager with Will being a shotgun blast away from Alex of being her next victim.  There had been a time when Morton Blackwell, Luis Moreno, and Will Bennett had sat down and talked about whether the firm should even go on.  Will was the most vulnerable of the three of them without much of a book of his own clients, but Morton and Luis had said they were staying in and Will did too.  Johnston & Blackwell survived and prospered and grew in large part because Luis and Morton had believed in Will Bennett.  Now Luis was sick and Morton needed his help.

Of all of life's values, to Will, loyalty was the most important.  When he played it all out, there really was only one answer:  Go back to Albuquerque and try the bejesus out of the case that Luis had taken on.

After that, he would sit down and reconsider his life and what he wanted to do with the rest of it.  He slept easy that night.

# CHAPTER TEN
## MAKING PLANS

The next morning Will met Morton for breakfast at Gary's, the locals' favorite hang out.

Will agreed that he would return and try the case assuming the client agreed. From Morton's perspective, that wasn't a problem. There wasn't anybody else to try it. For the next three weeks Will would stay in Michigan and prepare the file for trial. No one, as in no one, was to know that he was coming back except for Morton, Liz, Jackie and Rosalind McManus. As far as everyone else in the firm and the community were concerned, Rosalind would be trying her first big case. What nobody would know was that she would second chair it with Will. A week out from trial, Will would travel back to Albuquerque. Where he would stay was a problem that was solved when Morton offered up his in-laws' carriage house that had been made into guest quarters years ago but was rarely used.

"You want to at least check with them, Morton? Just asking." Morton's in-laws were most influential in the greater Albuquerque area and his father-in-law was the former mayor of the city. The guest quarters were big enough to house the control center for the trial.

"They'll be fine with it, Will. But I'll check."

Obviously, once the trial started, everybody would know Will Bennett was back, but there wasn't anything to do about that. It was Will's sincere hope that he could keep where he was staying a secret from almost everybody. Will also knew he would be followed by the inevitable gossip about Alex Kennedy and Don Jenkins and how he had had to leave town because of it, but that also couldn't be avoided. What happened after the trial would be left until after the trial.

Will revisited the decision he had made the previous night. He owed it to Luis and Morton to put aside his own bullshit and man up. He didn't relish trying the case against Roy McDaniels, but he had always hated bullies and now was as good a time as any to take one on.

He asked Morton to call Jackie on his way to the airport and have her scan the mediation briefs as well as the briefs that were filed when the defendant tried to get out on motion. He also wanted the court's order denying the motion. They hugged in the parking lot and Morton left for Grand Rapids. Will drove back to the lake house filled with a strange sense of excitement and exhilaration that he hadn't felt in a long time. By the time he got back, Jackie had already sent what he needed via email with the subject line: 'Welcome back.'

For the rest of the day, Will absorbed himself in the Ruiz file. His initial reaction was that it was a miracle the case had survived the defendant's motion, but the more he read the more he understood why Luis Moreno of all lawyers had taken the case. Luis liked to tilt at windmills and this was one hell of a windmill.

By all accounts, Felipe Ruiz had been a loser from his first day in this world. Born in the South Valley of Albuquerque to a single mom with six other children by five different fathers, Ruiz had quickly gravitated to the gang life that permeated that part of Albuquerque. By the time he was eighteen, he was living on the streets and had an arrest record a mile long of offenses of ever increasing violence. He was heavily tattooed, an intimidating man to be avoided at all costs. At the age of 32 he had killed a man who probably deserved it, but the judge and jury took umbrage at the fact that, after Ruiz had stabbed the man to death, he had cut him into little pieces and threw them into the Rio Grande. Unfortunately, while the stabbing had gone undetected, the mutilation part had been witnessed by a class of middle schoolers and their teachers on a field trip to explore the river bank flora. Because the students were still on the bus at the time, Ruiz didn't know he'd been spotted. The horrified bus driver kept driving and the teacher sitting in front stabbed in 911 on her cell phone as fast as she could. The police arrived just as the last parts of Ruiz's victim were disappearing into the brown water of the Rio Grande and the children were being bused back to school for traumatic stress counseling.  The jury found him guilty of second degree murder which was testament to the character of the victim and he was sentenced to nine years.  He was sent to PNM North, the supermax penitentiary on the Turquoise Trail south of Santa Fe.

It was at the North facility that Ruiz had gotten his first break in life.  In an attempted escape by a small group of particularly violent prisoners, he had been in the right place at the right time.  By killing two of the gang trying to escape, he had saved the life of a young guard who was being held hostage.  He had used a homemade shiv that he had carefully designed and constructed for self-defense, a fact overlooked by the prison warden and parole board.  After serving seven years, at age 39, Felipe Ruiz was a free man with no education and no skills to speak of – unless the design and construction of homemade shivs was considered a skill.  Incredibly, when he collected his meager belongings at his release, the shiv was among them.

Felipe Ruiz returned to Albuquerque and immediately went back to his roots, the South Valley where he grew up.  And that is when he got his second break.  He stopped at a Garcia's Restaurant on his way back to nowhere and was waited on by a woman about his age whose weary smile welcomed him to his booth.  Whether it was the years in prison or the weariness of her smile or a little of both, he struck up a conversation with her.  It was quiet in the restaurant that night, near closing time, and she had time to spare for him.  Painfully shy around women all his life, Ruiz asked her out and she, just as shyly, said yes.

There were some logistical problems.  He had no place to live, no transportation, and only what the great state of New Mexico had given him for money when he left North.  That night he slept on a park bench and the next day rented a room in a flophouse in the Valley.  It wasn't much but it was a bed.  He went looking for work and found a company called AAA Excavation that was looking for day laborers. He signed on and was surprised that no questions were asked about his background until he met the other laborers. If they weren't as violent as he had been, they were damn close.

The work was backbreaking and exhausting. Most of the workers' time was spent with shovels and pick axes, building a sewer line in the Corrales area northwest of Albuquerque. The foremen were little more than slave overseers who constantly insulted and berated the laborers to work harder and longer. The men got a ten minute break in the morning and afternoon and twenty minutes for lunch. In all respects, it was a chain gang made up of losers like Felipe Ruiz and run like one, only with meaner bosses.

But Felipe had enough time and energy to get to know Rosie Herrera and for her to get to know him. They began to see each other when time and opportunity permitted. She was a single mom raising two kids: an eighteen-year old named Jorge, with legal troubles himself, and a fifteen-year old girl, Yolanda, who was doing everything she could to escape from her mother's life to get to a better one.

Implausibly, Rosie and Felipe fell in love and he moved out of his rooming house and into her one-bedroom, one bath apartment. Ruiz got Jorge Herrera a job with AAA Excavation, and they worked side by side for the next several weeks under ever-deteriorating weather conditions as the New Mexico monsoon season ramped up. A month before his death, Rosie and Felipe were married in a simple civil ceremony at the courthouse. Will was startled to see that the officiating judge was none other than his wife.

AAA Excavation was way behind schedule and pushing its men harder and harder to make up the time. If it had been on schedule, the excavation work would have been done long before the monsoons that can turn dry creek beds into roaring rivers in a matter of minutes.  But it wasn't, and the bosses were determined to get the work finished regardless of the weather and the danger to their workers.  Two men had already almost lost their lives when the foremen had ordered them into the excavation site in the midst of a downpour.  There had been a cave in and the men had been rescued, but it had been a very close call.  Nothing changed.

Then, a little over a year after he was paroled, on August 16, Felipe Ruiz was one of a four man crew working on a part of the excavation that was particularly fragile because of the steepness of the slope.  The other three were his stepson, Jorge, an Anglo kid who looked a little crazy and who answered only to Ace, and another Hispanic young man named Rami.  The foreman ordered Ruiz into the ditch even though it was pouring and clear to all that a cave in was all but inevitable.  Ruiz had protested, telling the foreman that he was being sent to his death.  He was ordered into the pit anyway.  "No fuckin' ex-con spic murderer tells me what I can or can't do."

In another time and with a different Felipe Ruiz, he might simply have walked off the job, but he had Rosie and the kids to support.  Maybe he felt some macho sense to go into the ditch because Jorge was there.  They'd never know.  He took his shovel and climbed down.

Ruiz hadn't been in the deep ditch longer than three or four minutes when both sides collapsed on him.  His shoulders and head remained above the mud and water but everything else was buried.  While the foreman watched with what almost looked like a smile on his face, Jorge and the other two members of the crew worked feverishly to free Felipe.  But their attempts were futile and they could only watch in horror as the mud and water rose higher and higher until he was completely buried.

The last words Felipe Ruiz ever said were to Jorge were, "Tell your momma I love her."

And then he was gone.

Incredibly, the foreman ordered the men back to work telling Jorge they would pick up the 'spic's body' at the end of the day.  Jorge thought about killing the foreman then and there with the pick axe that he was holding, but instead he simply dropped it and walked off the job site.  It fell to him to tell his mother what had happened to her new husband.

Rosie Herrera did nothing.  She hid her grief as best she could and went back to Garcia's with her same weary smile.  The family received meager death benefits from the worker's compensation carrier which did little to change their lives.

But while Rosie accepted her loss much as she had accepted other losses in her life, Jorge would not be so passive.  He had come to love Felipe Ruiz in the short time he had known him and knew that if something didn't change, he would end up just like him - dead in the bottom of an excavation ditch or dead at the hands of a gang or doing hard time at North.  So he promised himself that he would change and he did.  He started on his GED, got a minimum wage job at a gas station, and worked his ass off.

And he went to see a lawyer.  The first four lawyers told him he didn't have a case.  Then somehow somewhere he heard about a Hispanic lawyer named Luis Moreno.  This time Jorge Herrera caught a break.

Will felt exhausted and disgusted when he finished reading. He knew why Luis had taken the case and he knew that he would do the best he could to get justice for this family.

In the days to come, Jackie sent mountains of material over the internet and Will devoured it all.  Luis had gone on a rampage seeking all of AAA Excavation's records that Roy McDaniels resisted at every turn.  But Luis was persistent and patient and it had paid off in a sickening treasure trove of materials.  AAA Excavation had been around for about ten years and was owned by a West Texas man by the name of Harry Conway.  Throughout its existence, AAA had bid state and federal excavating contracts and had quickly built a booming business in New Mexico.  It had also built a reputation as a ruthless employer whose injury rate was triple that of the competition which, for reasons unknown, had flown below state and federal investigative radars.  At its core, AAA depended on five foremen recruited by Conway from his days in the Texas oil fields who were known for their brutality and harshness in dealing with their work force.  Conway and his men were all Anglos and they depended on an overwhelmingly Hispanic work force made up of day laborers, homeless men, and, like Felipe Ruiz, ex-cons.

Statements under oath given by Harry Conway and the foremen of AAA Excavation took days, mostly because Roy McDaniels couldn't hear a question from Luis that wasn't objectionable.  Again, Luis's persistence and patience had paid off and the transcripts built a huge framework of indifference, meanness, and greed that was both outrageous and compelling. Whether it was enough to ultimately beat a  motion to dismiss had been the biggest concern, but Judge Del Rio had ruled that Luis had found enough evidence to send the case to the jury.

The Delgado doctrine was a result of a case brought on behalf of the Estate of Junior Delgado who was killed after he had been ordered to remove molten slag from a 15 foot high caldron in an emergency situation, even though he had never done that job before and had no training in how to do it.  Seven years before Felipe's death, the New Mexico Supreme Court had ruled that when an employer intentionally inflicts or willfully causes injury or death to its employee, it may not use the exclusivity provisions of the New Mexico Workers' Compensation Act to bar recovery in an action against it.  And so the Ruiz case was going to the jury.

After getting through all of the transcripts of the statements, numerous discovery motions to get the documents, and the rest of the legal briefs, Will had a telephone conference with Liz, Jackie, and Rosalind.  They went over potential jury instructions, the contents of the trial brief,  and they began to brainstorm voir dire questions for the jury panel.  They would get the jury questionnaires the Friday before trial and would have the weekend to sift through them.  Roy McDaniels had buried them with a series of pretrial motions designed to keep out the most damaging testimony about AAA Excavation as being too prejudicial.

'Of course it was prejudicial,' Will thought to himself.  'That's why you had trials.'  Jackie, as a third year law review student, took the lead on the responses to the motions, and Will marveled at the clarity and persuasiveness of her writing.  Jackie LaPointe had been a godsend to Johnston & Blackwell from the day she started.  Will and Alex had first met her when she was working as a techie with the Alexandria Police Department and then, months later, she had in effect shown up on their doorstep in Albuquerque looking for a new path for her life.  She had started as a gopher for the firm, worked up to running IT, and then became office manager, replacing the woman who had tried to kill Will and was instead shot by Alex.  In the meantime, she had started law school and, only six months before, had married an anesthesiology resident at the UNM Hospital.

His second chair, Rosalind McManus, was the Legal Services lawyer Alex had found at a conference and told Will about.  Mature beyond her years, she had quickly become the heir apparent to the litigation that Will and Luis handled for the firm and had easily and without complaint taken on Will's files when he left for Michigan.  She was attractive, charming, tough, and unflappable even in the face of a McDaniels tirade of which she had been the target many times during the workup of the Ruiz case.  She was ready and spoiling for a fight.  Luis had once described her as having ice in her veins.  Will agreed.


On a Friday in August, ten days before trial, Will shut down the lake house and packed his car.  The night before he had had dinner at the locals' favorite restaurant with Rusty, Dan, Reba

Sue, and Grace.  It had been a special time with lots of laughter mostly at Will's expense ('Shit' was the theme of the party).  Rusty and Dan gave Will a Leatherman belt tool that bristled with knives, screwdrivers, and saws.  It was, according to them, all Will ever needed to build whatever he wanted.  Scratched into the side was the word 'shit.'

Grace planned to spend the night, and when they got home, Will poured himself an Irish and Grace a glass of wine.  They went out on the deck and sat in the recliners looking at the millions of stars in the clear night.

"You going to see Alex when you get back, Dad?"

"I'm not sure, honey.  What do you think?"

"I think yes.  Alex and I have talked a lot over these last few weeks.  I'm not sure you knew that."

"How would I have?"

"I don't know.  Intuition?"

They both laughed.  Like men had any sense of intuition when it came to women.

"I'm glad you're going back."

"Me too, I guess.  Although it has been great here."

"I know but it's not you.  At least not yet."

"I know."

The next morning they hugged and hugged and then Grace got in her car back to her life in Grand Rapids and Will got into his car back to his life in Albuquerque, whatever that would look like.  The Leatherman tool hung proudly on his belt.

This time he took two full days to drive it.  His head was a jumble of Alex, Grace, and mostly the Ruiz case.  He worked on themes and theories for the case, tried a bunch and discarded most of them.  He represented the Estate of Felipe Ruiz who for almost all of his life had been a very bad man.  And while the heirs of his estate, Rosie and her two kids, would be the ones who would recover anything if there were anything to recover, Felipe's past would be a major presence in the trial.

Somewhere in Oklahoma it began to come together for him.  This wasn't about who Felipe had been, it was about who he was when he died.  It wasn't about his violent past or his years in prison, it was about trying to make a life for Rosie and her kids with no skills and no education and no option but to work for men like Harry Conway and his henchmen.

It was about a life of redemption.

And by eastern New Mexico, it came to him that that was what his life and Alex's life were all about.  Redemption.

To say that Morton Blackwell's in-laws' carriage house was stunningly beautiful was an understatement.  Set on a multi-acre ranch north of Albuquerque, large picture windows faced east to the Sandias, and out the front porch was a beautiful corral and meadows with August wildflowers covering the ground.  Morton's in-laws were away touring Europe, so other than the man who ran the place from day to day, Will and his team were alone.  They met Monday morning amidst much joy at seeing each other again.  It was a happy homecoming for Will in many ways.  The group moved boxes and boxes into the living room of the carriage house that was bigger than anything Will had ever lived in.  They put away the groceries, organized files and began brainstorming.  The team voted unanimously for redemption as the theme and began to work the voir dire, the opening statement, and the witness exams around it.

Two weeks before, Will had come to the conclusion that Roy McDaniels was likely to send the whole AAA crew off to the Bahamas for a nice vacation, so he hired a process server and subpoenaed Conway and the five foremen before they could get away.  He had them all.

That Monday afternoon, Will, Liz, Jackie, and Rosalind met with Rosie Herrera (now Ruiz), Jorge, and Yolanda at a little restaurant south of town.  Will had been worried about Rosie because McDaniels had tried to brutalize her in her statement under oath, but her sad eyes and that weary smile belied a courage that was almost animal like.  She would see it through.  Jorge was the executor of his stepfather's estate and was both a huge liability and huge damage witness.  He too had been brutalized at his statement but, since Felipe's death, he had finished his GED and was enrolled at the community college in Albuquerque.  His dream?  To become a lawyer and help people like Luis Moreno had helped him.  Yolanda, whose deposition had not been taken, was starting her senior year in high school and had already received academic scholarship offers from several colleges and universities.  She would pick UNM to be close to her mom.

They went over where they were and what the trial would look like.  Jackie would take them over to the courthouse to see Judge Del Rio's courtroom and Rosie and Jorge had transcripts of their statements to read and study ahead of trial.  As they said good bye, Rosie gave Will a hug and thanked him for being there for the family.  He hugged her back and told her they would do the best they could.

"That's all I can ask, Will."  That weary smile again.

Monday evening, Morton and Will went to see Luis at his house.  His doctors had put off the bypass operation for now and Luis was in the process of having more tests done.  Stents were a possible option and far less intrusive than bypass surgery.  Luis was overwhelmed to see them both.  Morton had kept his word and had not told Luis that Will was coming back to try the case, and it was clear from Luis' face that a load had been taken off his shoulders.

"This was murder, Will.  Pure and simple."

"I know it was, Luis, and we'll do everything we can to prove it."

They left it that Will would see Luis at least one or two more times to brainstorm the case ahead of next week's start.

That night Will slept better than he had in weeks.


The next days and nights were filled with trial preparation and file organization.  Will and Rosalind met with Luis twice during the week and Luis agreed that redemption was a great theme.  He also concurred that it was "all or nothing" in terms of the burden of proof and that Will would call each of the AAA men as witnesses as the first order of business.  With the documents that had reluctantly been produced over McDaniels' objections, and with the admissions Luis had gotten from each of them at their sworn statements, there was at least a very circumstantial case that could be made that Felipe Ruiz might as well have been murdered given what was done to him.

On Friday, Rosalind McManus argued the various motions that McDaniels had filed in his attempt to keep out evidence and she won every one of them.  Judge Del Rio had heard too many defense motions in the case and clearly had had enough of Roy McDaniels.  That was a plus.

Liz picked up the juror questionnaires filled out by the potential jurors and they pored over them on Saturday morning. They liked the pool, and each prospective juror was assigned a Post-It Note with the name and any relevant information written on it so they could keep track as jurors were questioned. On Sunday, other than tinkering with the questions Will would ask the potential jurors during the selection process, and the opening statement language, and meeting with the family one more time, the trial team rested.  They couldn't be any more ready.

Will Bennett, the rest of the trial team, and the Ruiz family entered Judge Del Rio's courtroom thirty minutes ahead of the 8:30 start time to set up. They had met at the offices of Johnston & Blackwell, loaded up the boxes, and headed out.

Shortly after they arrived in court, Roy McDaniels and three associates, along with Harry Conway and five very rough looking men, walked in and began to set up at their table. As a matter of courtesy, Will walked over to introduce himself to McDaniels. They shook hands perfunctorily.

"I'm surprised to see you here, Will Bennett. Everybody I know thought Don Jenkins ran you out of town after he fucked your wife."

"Everybody thought wrong, Roy." They stared at each other for a moment, let the testosterone bubble, and Will turned back to counsel table. Game on.

At promptly 8:30 the bailiff entered the courtroom, said "All rise," and Judge Del Rio took the bench noting with a nod that Will Bennett was at counsel table.

"Anything we need to go over before I bring the panel in?"
Will. "No, Your Honor."
McDaniels. "No, Your Honor."
"Bailiff, if you would be so kind."

From the moment the jury panel was ushered into the courtroom to the time the jury reached a verdict, four and a half days passed. Most trials have ebbs and flows in which something good will happen to one side and then something good will happen to the other but this case was a little different. Realizing that the Court of Appeals might well reverse any verdict because AAA Excavation was Mr. Ruiz's employer and because the family had received worker's compensation benefits, Will and his team held nothing back. Harry Conway was the first witness Will called, and by the time he was done with him two things had happened.  The jury hated Harry Conway for his conceit and his smugness and hated Roy McDaniels even more.

The five foremen followed in turn and each gave up admission after admission of the horrible way AAA Excavation treated its workers.  Will ended with "Arkansas Slim" Baker who was the man who ordered Felipe Ruiz into the ditch knowing it was a near certainty to cave in given the heavy rains.  While Baker didn't get all the way to admitting he knew he was sending Felipe to his death, he came close.  He testified that he may have said something like "no fuckin' ex-con spic murderer tells me what I can or can't do."  And he may have said something like "we'll get the spic's body later, keep working," but he couldn't be sure.  But even if he did say those things, he didn't mean anything by it.  That didn't play well to anybody on a New Mexico jury, especially one that had three Hispanic people on it like this one did.

Unfortunately for "Arkansas Slim" and AAA Excavation, every other member of the work crew that day was sure he had said those things and had meant every word.

As the trial progressed, Will noticed that Roy McDaniels was looking less and less well.  His already florid face was taking on a purple hue, it was dotted with perspiration, and he was drinking an inordinate amount of water at counsel table. His clothing was more and more disheveled.  Even his associates looked concerned.

Rosalind put Rosie Ruiz on the stand and she was incredibly powerful in talking about her love for Felipe and the loss she felt when he was gone.  McDaniels tried to bully her into talking about Felipe's past and she would have none of it.  If the jury hadn't hated him before then, trying to bully the widow was not going to help.  Yolanda Herrera was next and she spoke of the conversations she had had with Felipe in which he made her promise over and over again that she would finish school and go to college so she didn't end up like him.  Even McDaniels was smart enough to leave her alone.

Plaintiff's case ended with Jorge Herrera.  Will questioned him about his life and his own troubles with the law, the addition of Felipe Ruiz to their family, the work that Felipe did with Jorge to get him straightened out, the job with AAA Excavation, the day of his step-father's death, and what "Arkansas Slim" told Ruiz. After all that, Will had one last question for Jorge: "What was the last thing Felipe Ruiz said before he died?"

" 'Tell your momma I love her.' "

There was not a dry eye on the jury or anywhere else in the courtroom save for those sitting at the defense table.

"Your witness."

McDaniels stood up to cross examine, looked at the jury, looked at Jorge, looked at Will, and sat back down.

"No questions, Your Honor."  Jorge Ruiz was excused.

The defense called no witnesses having tried to rehabilitate the AAA Excavation witnesses after Will had examined them as a part of the plaintiff's case.  If the defense had any chance, it would have to be based on law and not fact.

Throughout the course of the trial, Will and his team had noticed three strangers in the courtroom who attended the trial each day, sat on the defense side, and took pages of notes for each witness.  They had no idea who they were.

There was a fourth stranger who sat on the plaintiff's side, a young African American man who sat quietly alert through the whole trial and never engaged with anybody until Jackie LaPointe stopped him in the hallway during a recess and introduced herself. His name was Ricky Storm, and when Jackie asked him why he was interested in the trial he told her that he was the prison guard whose life had been saved when Felipe Ruiz had killed two of the men who were holding him hostage.  All he said to her was, "This is where I need to be." Jackie had seen enough of life to know exactly what he meant.

Closing arguments were Will's favorite part of a trial and this case was no exception. He started with his theme of redemption, wove it through the argument, accused AAA Excavation of nothing less than premeditated murder, told the jury what Rosie, Yolanda, and Jorge had lost, and sat down. Roy McDaniels let one of his associates do the closing argument that truly was nothing more than a plea for leniency. It was mercifully short. Rebuttal was brutal and Will Bennett left no room for the jury to do anything other than bring justice for the life of Felipe Ruiz so that he hadn't died in vain. He told the jury that Rosie, Yolanda, and Jorge would be waiting. When he was done, he turned to walk back to counsel table and saw Alex Kennedy in the back of the courtroom. His heart skipped, he sat down, and thought he was going to faint.

The court read the jury instructions that contained the language about intentional wrongdoing, gross negligence, and willful and wanton misconduct that was AAA Excavation's only hope, and the jury was sent to deliberate. They were out an hour and a half.

As the bailiff ushered them back in, each one looked at Rosie Ruiz as they took their seats.

Judge Del Rio. "Would the foreperson please rise?"

A middle aged woman, an Hispanic homemaker who had taken page after page of notes during the trial, stood.

"Have you reached a verdict?"

"We have, Your Honor."

The night of the verdict, Roy McDaniels died of a massive heart attack in his office after having consumed an entire bottle of single malt Scotch.  Will Bennett hoped his death wasn't because as he was leaving the courtroom, he had walked past McDaniels and said: "Tell everybody who thinks I was run out of town because Don Jenkins fucked my wife that I'm back."

He just couldn't help himself and he didn't feel one ounce of remorse for having said it.

The verdict?  $3.7 million in compensatory damages and $15 million in punitive damages.  It would be a long time before Rosie, Jorge, and Yolanda saw any of it, if ever, but it was a pretty good start.  It turned out that the three strangers in the courtroom taking notes were a state investigator, a federal investigator, and an insurance adjustor.  On his way out of the courtroom, Ricky Storm shook Will's hand and thanked him for what he had done.  He turned next to Jackie who was behind Will, put his arms around her, and with tears rolling down his cheeks said only, "He got justice, Jackie, and you got it for him.  Thank you."  And then he turned and was gone.

The team spent time with the family after the verdict.  They were overwhelmed not so much by the amount of money the jury awarded, but that Felipe Ruiz's life had been given dignity and worth.  That meant everything to them.

Liz wondered about the Coppertop to celebrate but Will declined.  Still too many bad memories there.  So they adjourned to the carriage house to debrief and enjoy the aftermath.  Luis had been in the courtroom when the jury came back and he joined them as well.  Johnston & Blackwell had kicked some major butt in this trial.  They knew it as a team, and the rest of the community, legal and otherwise, would know it soon enough.

Will Bennett wondered about Alex being in the courtroom.

A week later, three days after a very sparse turnout for Roy McDaniels' funeral that Will missed, a joint state and federal investigation was announced targeting AAA Excavation, and why, with such an abysmal safety record, it had been awarded so many municipal, state, and federal contracts.

A Motion for a Judgment Notwithstanding the Verdict and a Motion for New Trial were filed and denied summarily by Judge Del Rio. An appeal was timely filed by what was left of Roy McDaniels' firm but, shortly after that, the file was transferred to another firm to handle the appeal. The briefing schedule was set and Jackie would take the lead on drafting the reply. It was going to be a risk given the state of the law. Everybody, including Rosie, Jorge, and Yolanda, knew it. For those three, though, the verdict of twelve strangers had been enough.

Two weeks later, McDaniels and Associates closed its doors and let the bank take back what fixtures and furniture it could get its hands on. The *Albuquerque Tribune* reported that McDaniels personally and his firm had been mired in overwhelming debt at the time of his last verdict. When he heard the news, Will Bennett felt nothing, an emotion shared sadly by all who had known McDaniels.

# CHAPTER FOURTEEN
## SUMMIT CONFERENCE

On the Sunday after the verdict, a high level conference of emissaries was held at Seasons Restaurant in the Old Town neighborhood of Albuquerque. Attendees were Karen Stillson, Liz LaRue and Jackie LaPointe and the topic was how to get Alex and Will back together. Unfortunately, they didn't get to what they needed to get to until they had ordered their second round of drinks, and by then the conversation had deteriorated somewhat. Handcuffs, blind dates, spiked brownies, get-away vacations where they ended up in the same location, handcuffs, emergency phone calls to each other, and handcuffs were some of the ideas.

"Jesus, Liz, lay off the handcuffs, OK?

"Sorry. Been on my mind lately."

"It's OK. Really. It just won't work here. But you go for it. Really."

The emissaries needn't have worried.

Will was sitting on the porch of the carriage house thinking about what to do next. The trial was over and he had fulfilled his commitment to the firm and his promise to Luis. Technically, he was still on a leave of absence. He could pack his bags, go back to Michigan, and start the process all over again. He had to admit it had been good to be back in trial, it had been good to be back with the trial team, and it was good to be back in Albuquerque. And Alex had been in the courtroom to watch the closing argument.

If he stayed in New Mexico, he'd have to find a place to live and he thought about the hassles of doing that. He could get an apartment but then he'd have to find furniture and pots and pans and all that other crap that went with living alone. He was too old for that. Plus, if he stayed, the ghost of Alex Kennedy would be forever present and what had gone on between the two of them would always be a part of his life. He was not at all sure he could handle that.

But if he went back to Michigan he'd have to do the same thing about a place to stay, at least in the winter.  And God, the gray of Michigan winters.  Why would he do that to himself?  Grace was the biggest reason to go back.  So there he sat, deep in thought, mulling over the next chapter.

A familiar car drove down the driveway.  Will felt his pulse spike and he got a little short of breath.  The car pulled to a stop in front of the porch and Alex Kennedy stepped out holding a bottle of wine.  Will stood up as she walked up the steps and they stopped a couple of feet from each other.
"Hey, Will."
"Hey, Alex."
"Congrats on the trial."
"Thanks. It's over.  That's the main thing."
"Winning's better than losing," she smiled.
"Yes, it is," and he smiled back.
"I love you, Wilson Bennett."
"I love you, Alexandra Kennedy."
In the years to come, neither of them would ever really understand what happened next or even agree on what happened next.  They did agree that, at some point, there was the shedding of clothing and holding each other that took their breath away, and a hunger for each other they hadn't felt since those first many many times they'd been together.  They both remembered not talking but a lot of action.  And tears.  And laughter.  And somehow, some way, there was a purity and a freshness and an honesty and a clarity to being together again.
Morning came and neither had slept a minute.  They had talked some about the little stuff of life but mostly they had left the past and the future alone.  Alex got up and dressed and Will made them coffee and toast.  They sat on the back deck and watched the morning light begin to rise over the Sandias.
"Will I see you again, Alex?"
"Do you want to?"
"Not so fast.  You go first."
"I hope so."
"Me, too."

She kissed him goodbye, got in her car, and left.  He went back inside, poured another cup of coffee and began a slow dance around the kitchen loosely performed to the tune of *My Girl* hummed under his breath.  For her part, she had a shit-eating grin on her face all the way home to change and all the way to the courthouse.

She walked into her chambers and found Karen Stillson in some disarray.

"You OK, Karen?"

"Sorry, Judge, may have gotten a little overserved last night.  Maybe."

"Feeling a tad fragile, are we?" Alex accompanied the comment with a huge smile.  "Hope you feel better."  And went whistling into her inner office.

Karen Stillson immediately went to her email and sent the following to Jackie and Liz: 'Something happened.'

Not very many blocks away, Will Bennett walked into the office of Johnston & Blackwell with his own shit-eating grin on his face.  Cheerily said good morning to a new receptionist and walked down the hall to his office.  He passed both Liz and Jackie who had just heard from Karen and gave them both a hug.  Both immediately went back to their respective work stations and emailed Karen back:

Jackie: 'We know.  We think it's good.'

Liz: 'Think it was the handcuffs?'

Except for the first morning of the trial a week ago, it was the first time Will had been back at the firm in weeks.  He spent much of the morning reconnecting with people he cared so much about and catching up on news about the firm and the community.

Around 11, Morton walked into his office.

"I've got some good news, I think.  My in-laws don't get back until mid-September and my wife, Socorro, emailed them and they said you could stay as long as you want."  He looked at Will for a second.

"You OK?"

"Never better.  Thanks, Morton, that means a lot."

"That mean you're staying around for a while?  With Luis still out, we've got plenty of work."

"I'm working through it, Morton.  Thanks again."

Morton left Will's office and immediately headed for Liz LaRue.

"What's up with Will?"

She smiled.  "Not sure but we think it's good news."

He walked down the hall to his own office smiling for the first time in weeks.

Meanwhile, Will was in his office having another adolescent moment in terms of what to do next.  Should he call? Should he text? Should he email?  Should he do nothing and let it all sit?  So he punted and called his daughter who thankfully was in her office.

"Dad!  I just got off the phone with Alex and she said you guys had a date last night.  That is so cool!"  He thought to himself that his generation would never have called last night a date but what the hell.

"We had a very nice time, Grace."

"So, when do you see each other again?  Soonly?"  An old joke between father and daughter.

"Not sure.  I hope so."

"Well, not to give away secrets, but she sure hopes it's soon.  She sounded very excited." A pause.  "Although kind of tired at the same time, if you know what I mean?"

Will stifled a yawn.

"I think so.  Well, maybe I'll give her a call and see how she is.  Whadda you think?"

"Perfect, Dad.  I'm so proud of you guys.  Talk to you soon. I love you, Dad."

Proud of us?  Hah, if she only knew about her old man and her stepmother.  Now that was something to be proud of.  Armed with the courage of his daughter's enthusiasm, he dialed Alex's direct line into her chambers.  She picked up on the first ring.

"Hi."

"Hi.  You told Grace we had a date last night?  That's what you think it was?"

Alex laughed that laugh he loved so much that came deep from her diaphragm.

"Rutting like crazed weasels seemed like a little too much information for your daughter."

It was Will's turn to laugh.

"Always the diplomat.  How are you?"

"Beyond exhaustion and never better.  You?"

"Exactly there.  Want to get a glass of wine sometime?"

"Sure.  Tonight would be great."  Had somebody walked in the room?  "Let's do 5:30.  Great to hear from you."  Somebody better have goddamned walked into her chambers and it had better not have been a certain district judge.

An email came through:  'Sorry.  Settlement conference attendees with no manners.  Let's do the townhouse.  There are a couple of cats who would like to say hello.'"  He emailed back:  'I'll be there and bring some wine and munchies.'  In return:  'Got some Irish that's getting old, too.  And a hot tub that needs some use.'

Will got nothing done the rest of the day.  A number of people tried to engage him but all he could do was giggle when anybody would say anything.  The one exception was when the *Albuquerque Tribune* reporter, Megan Dixon, called for a comment on the verdict which was one of the largest personal injury verdicts in the history of Bernalillo County.  He had known Megan over the years and she had covered several of his larger cases.  He liked her but told her he would have no comment, at least at this point.

"Off the record, Will?"

"Sure, Megan.  I don't mean to be difficult but this is really tragic."

"I know and I won't push for now as long as you give me the exclusive when your side is ready to talk."

"Of course."

"And Will?"

"Yup."

"Hell of a way to make an entrance.  Incredible verdict and you killed a dickhead of a lawyer in the process."  He laughed.

"Off the record, if it holds up on appeal I'll have the trifecta."

Megan's turn to laugh.

"Congratulations, Will, and welcome back.  This community is the better for it."

Out of nowhere, he teared up for a second.  There was a hesitancy in his voice as he replied,

"Thanks Megan.  Means a lot."

"Down the road, dude, and don't forget the exclusive.  Bye."

He heard from a number of other colleagues that afternoon, mostly by email, congratulating him on the win.  It had been big news starting Friday night and continuing through the weekend, compounded of course by the fact that Roy McDaniels had dropped dead within hours of the verdict.

One colleague emailed: 'Whoa, talk about taking it hard.'

Another: 'Should I feel something? Sounds like a good outcome all the way around.'

Another: 'Congrats.  Even better, good to have you back.'

Several others like that.  Nice job and glad you're back.

Will got back to thinking what he had been thinking in Michigan.  Was working as a lawyer what he wanted to do for the rest of his career?  He was proud of what he had accomplished for his clients but, like McDaniels, he had lost some doozies in his day.  He hadn't done it being the prick that McDaniels had been, and maybe that was the difference, but still, how many more trials were there and should there be?  He had come back out of loyalty to Luis and Morton.  And then Will laughed at himself.  Yeah, that was true.  But what was even more true was that he had come back for Alex.

At promptly 5:30 he knocked on the townhouse door.  There was no need to tell Alex that he had driven around aimlessly for 20 minutes to kill time because he was so excited to be seeing her again, or that he had called eight wine stores to find one that carried Frog's Leap that was their favorite wine drunk only on very special occasions, or that he had spent a half hour in the deli section looking for cheeses that he knew she would like.

And there was no reason why Will should know that her settlement conference had ended early with the judge declaring an impasse when there really wasn't one quite yet. Or that he should know she'd been home for an hour cleaning the house, showering and figuring out what to wear.  Or that she had stopped at the Monte Carlo and bought the most expensive Irish whiskey they carried. Or that she had gone to the grocery store to pick up creamed herring that was his favorite.

The irony?  From 3:30 to 5:30, they probably passed within feet of each other as they traversed the stores to make their time together special for each other.

Alex opened the door and immediately they were both overcome with a shyness that was  uncomfortable.  He was knocking at the door to the townhouse where he had lived for several years and now didn't.  He was being welcomed into a home that was no longer his and he was being introduced to cats that he had known and cared about for years.

Alex said it first.  "Well, this is pretty weird."

"Yup."

"Maybe we should have found some neutral ground for a while."

"Maybe."  Jesus Christ, Will, would you say something relevant or at the very least semi-interesting?

"We could go out."

"Yup."  About then Josie and Jinks appeared and, contrary to what they usually did when strangers appeared, walked up to Will for a good smell.

"Should we?"  He leaned down, held out his hands, and Josie crawled right into them.

"Nope." Alex nodded.

"Can I pour you a drink?  I got some special Irish."

"OK.  You too?"

"I will.  Will, let me take the bag.  Wow! Frog's Leap! Special occasion?"

What he wished to come out as "I hope so" sounded even to him like an immature frog in the spring clearing its throat.

Alex laughed, took the bag, and put the cheese and the wine in the fridge.

"Let's you and me get an Irish, be together just the two of us, and take it slow."  She paused for effect.  "At least until you can speak a language I can understand."  She laughed that laugh and he laughed and things got to be OK.  Sort of.

They spent the evening talking without the consuming passion of the night before.  That was all right for both of them because they were beginning to learn how to love each other again when they were together and not just longing for each other over massive distances.  There were some big things to talk about but neither was ready to do that.  They simply needed to be with each other after so long apart.  The big things would come later and they would get solved or not get solved.  But that was not for tonight.

Then there was a second glass of the best Irish either had ever had, then they opened the cheese and the herring, then they opened the Frog's Leap and got in the hot tub naked.  Without saying anything, both noticed their bodies had changed a bit for the better.  Alex knew enough about his life back in Michigan not to ask about the fingernails, two of which were showing signs of growing back.  They climbed out of the hot tub and showered and Alex asked if Will wanted to stay the night.  He really wanted to say no to make some stupid point but he had had two…or maybe three…Irish whiskeys, a large part of a very good bottle of wine, shared a hot tub with the beautiful love of his life, and hadn't slept in what seemed like days.  And he'd want to go back to the empty carriage house, why?

"Is it OK if I stay?"

"Wouldn't have asked if it wasn't, Will.  But can I ask you something personal?"

"Sure."

"Have you been seeing anybody?  Here?  Michigan?"

Will held up his left hand.  "Manuelita."  He held up the five fingers of his left hand.  "And her five sisters."  She smiled.

"How about you, Alex?"

She stood up, walked stiff-legged for the length of the room clapping her hands, then she turned around and walked the same way back to him.

They'd known each other too long.  "Energizer bunny?"

She nodded and they both smiled.

"Life is good then.  Let's go to bed, Will."

"Yup."  Will looked at his watch.  It was 7:30 and the sun was at least an hour from setting.  They went upstairs and pulled the blinds and were asleep, both of them, within seconds.  Spooned till morning.

Which meant 4:30 came around pretty quickly.  And that left only one option.

"Frontier?"

"Of course."


The Frontier, on Central across from the University of New Mexico, had been around forever and had served generations of cops, students, miscreants, community leaders and, in recent years, Alex and Will.  At five in the morning, there was a lull between drunken students and the change of shifts for the Albuquerque Police Department.  They placed their order for breakfast burritos and coffee, found a booth, and sat in silence until the food arrived.


"I think we should talk about some things, Will."  Very serious, especially for five in the morning.

"OK."

"I will never know why I did what I did.  I have never been so ashamed about anything I have ever done in my life."  She paused.  "And as you know, there were some things in the old days that I certainly should be ashamed of."  She smiled.

"You don't have to say any of this, Alex.  What's done is done."

"No, you're wrong.  I have to get this off my chest.  From the time you and I first met, you have been the only one, the only one that I ever wanted, ever needed, ever anything."  Tears now, which Will took as a sign of something but had no idea what.  "So then I go and throw it all away on a guy who was an asshole twenty years ago and who is still an asshole.  I didn't know why I did it when it happened and I still don't.  And neither does my therapist who frankly hasn't been very helpful because all she has ever said is 'that was a really stupid thing to do, Alex.'  I pay her to say things like that, right?" She stopped long enough to take a bite of burrito and that gave Will a chance to break in.

"You remember that time we went to that wedding back in Michigan years ago, before we were married, and the preacher told the couple the main thing was to pay attention to each other?" Alex nodded. "We talked about that a lot that night and promised each other we'd always pay attention. 'Member?" She nodded again. "I think that's where we got a little lost along the way, Alex. We forgot to pay attention to each other. Done a lot of thinking over the last weeks and I've come to a couple of conclusions. Want to hear them?"

On issues of the heart, this was about as long a speech as Will Bennett had ever made. She nodded for him to continue.

"The way we were going, running from day to day, going through all the stuff with Sam and the firm and the court and Grace, if it hadn't been you, it would have been me. That's the first thing. Second thing, what happened in the past is nothing compared to what we do today and tomorrow and tomorrow and tomorrow and for all the tomorrows we have left. That is what we need to talk about. You know what Robert said?"

Alex shook her head.

"At the end of the day, it's only body parts." They smiled remembering how much Robert had done for both of them.

Alex Kennedy and Will Bennett finished their breakfast in silence.

"So Will, what do we do with today and tomorrow and tomorrow and tomorrow and all the tomorrows we have left?"

"Right. That's the complicated part. I've thought about that too. You know what McDaniels said to me when we met in the courtroom?"

"No."

"Something to the effect of, 'Surprised to see you. Everybody I know thought Don Jenkins ran you out of town after he fucked your wife.'" Alex flinched.

"Know what I said to him on the way out of the courtroom after the trial?"

She shook her head.

"Tell everybody who thinks I was run out of town because Don Jenkins fucked my wife that I'm back."

A faint smile crossed her lips. "Wow."

"Yeah, hope that's not what killed him. So that's what's complicated. What about you and me and how do we do that if we really love each other? How do we deal with the rumors and gossip that now will rekindle if I stay? Do we live apart? Do we live together? Do you want more coffee?"

"Sure. Thanks." Will stood up and got the refills and sat back down.

"So, whadda you think? You're the Chief Judge of the Second Judicial  District Court. Whadda you want?"

She thought about it for a minute because she wanted to get it right.

"At the end of this plane of life, what we'll be known for is simple. It's all about the people we love and who love us. It's not about plaques or power or position. It's about us. And if we can't say 'fuck `em if they can't take a joke' and if the people we love won't stand with us with all our imperfections, then we're better off someplace else and doing something different. For me, I say we stand tall. You and I didn't get to where we are by running away."

She was right, of course. But he'd never faced pain like this before.

"You're right, of course. But I've never faced something like this before."

"You just hit the biggest asshole…may he rest in peace…for $18.7 million dollars. Pretty nice way to say you're back in town."

It was Will's turn to smile.

"Wining's better than losing."

"Are you back?"

"Gettin' there."

Will dropped Alex off at the townhouse.  As she got out of the car, she said, "You still have plenty of clothes here, you know."

"No Goodwill yet?"

"Never stopped hoping."

"Don't make any rash decisions.  Good thing I took that underwear when I left that can go six weeks without washing."

She made a face, closed the car door, and walked in the townhouse.

Will drove back to the carriage house, showered and shaved, and changed into something more casual than 'go to court' clothes.  He made sure the Leatherman was attached to his belt. You never know when you're gonna need it.  He got to work later than usual and found a note on his desk that Luis Moreno wanted to see him.  Luis?  He was supposed to be off work until the heart doctors figured out what to do with him.

He walked down to Luis' office, knocked on the closed door, and walked in to find Morton and Luis waiting for him.

"Luis, should you be here?  Really?"

"Everybody's got to be some place, Will.  Doctors tell me as long as nobody upsets me, I can do a little work.  That means you, Will.  Everything and everybody else is fine."

"Will, the reason we want to meet with you is to lay a guilt trip on you that is both unforgivable and impossible not to give in to.  You remember that time when the three of us met when all the shit was coming down…"

"No need for the guilt trip, Morton," Will interrupted. "I've thought a lot about this since you showed up back in Michigan and I have relived that meeting with the two of you a hundred times.  I know where I need to be and it's here.  I've thought a lot about what drove me out of here four months ago and I wondered how I would feel given what went down.  But a good friend said to me recently 'the people who love us will stand with us no matter what' or something like that.  The two of you stood with me when you didn't have to and I get, more than most, what that means.  If you'll have me back, I'm here."  They nodded.

"Alex?"  Luis and Morton spoke almost in unison.

"Gettin' there."  An inner smile lit him up from inside.  "Taking it a day at a time."

"Then we're good to go.  Let's get Rosalind, Jackie, Liz, and Rebecca together over lunch in the conference room and we'll figure out where we are on files."  Luis paused.  "Plus we've got to figure what we do with the twenty-seven calls we've gotten in since the verdict hit the media.  Turns out when Johnston & Blackwell hits a case for $18.7 million dollars, a lot of people want to find a good lawyer to take their case."

Will stood to leave.  "Thank you, gentlemen."  When he reached the door, a thought struck him and he turned back.

"Luis, you really did have a heart attack, didn't you?"

"Death's door, Will.  After all this time, how could you doubt me?"  He looked so hurt that Will instantly regretted saying anything.


But as he walked down the hall, he rethought the regret and started laughing out loud.  Goddamned trial lawyers.  When do you ever know if they're telling the truth?  And Will Bennett would never know for sure.  And it didn't matter one damn bit.  He was back.

He emailed Alex and told her about the meeting and what had been decided.

"Good.  If you need a washing machine, call me."

He called Rusty, got him at the work site, and filled him in on the trial and what had happened since and that he was going to stay in Albuquerque for the immediate future.  Unless Dan and Rusty needed him and he'd be back in a heartbeat.

Rusty laughed and laughed and then put him on speaker.

"Hey Dan, Will says he's gonna stay in Albuquerque unless we need him.  Whadda you think?"  Will could hear Dan laughing as hard as Rusty.

"You guys aren't exactly helping my ego much, you know."

He heard Rusty catch his breath.

"Dude, it's what, Dan?  A hundred times a day we don't say to each other 'damn, where's Will when we need him?'  At least a hundred times a day.  But somehow we're gettin' there without you."  He paused.  "Will, you are where you need to be.  Alex?"

"Gettin' there."

"Then all is good, my friend.  Fingernails?"

"Only lost two of them and they're growing back.  Rest seem to be hanging in."

"Good fingernails will do that.  When do we see you again?  Soon?"

"Not sure but I hope so.  Give my love to Reba Sue."

"Done.  Take care."

"Take care, Will."  Dan.

"Over and out."  And the connection was gone.

Next he called Robert back East, got his voice mail, and left the headlines.

A couple of minutes later he got a text: 'Can't talk now but I heard good things were in the offing.  Love to you both.'

Over deli sandwiches in the conference room, the litigation group went over existing cases, where they stood, what Will should take, what they could leave with Rosalind, and how to divide up Luis' case load, but that was almost the easy part.  What was really going to be a struggle was what they were going to do with all the phone calls that were coming in since the verdict.  Case selection was always one of the hardest parts of any plaintiffs' practice, and with the overload it would be doubly difficult.  The solution came to all of them almost at the same time.  Luis was going to have to take it easy for awhile and he and his assistant, Rebecca Jackson, who had been around forever, were the natural choices to screen the cases.

"'Course it would be nice if the two of you could find some cases we could actually win as opposed to tilting at windmills," Will noted.

"Right, Will, we only gave you and Rosalind an $18.7 million dollar verdict that was a lay down from the git-go," Rebecca replied.  "We'll try to do better in the future."

They all laughed and the meeting ended with Will thanking everybody for having him back.  That afternoon, files began appearing on Will's desk with complete memos on the status of the case signed off on by both Rosalind and Jackie.

CHAPTER SIXTEEN
HARRY CONWAY AND THE SAGA OF AAA
EXCAVATION

The *Albuquerque Tribune* reported on the federal and state investigation into AAA Excavation and its contracts with federal and state agencies.   An immediate result of the announcement of the investigation was the suicide of a contracting agent with the New Mexico Department of Transportation, an ominous sign for the future of AAA Excavation.

Johnston & Blackwell had already retained private investigators from Moretti & Moretti to do its own investigation of both AAA and, more importantly, its sole shareholder, Harry Conway.  With the promise of cooperation between the private investigators and the federal and state agencies, the investigation began.  While the focus of the government investigations was the relationship between the company and the governmental contracting authorities, the focus of Moretti & Moretti was whether Harry Conway had hidden money and where it was just in case the appellate courts affirmed the verdict.  AAA Excavation had insurance and had to be bonded in order to do the government work, but Will knew both the insurance company and the bonding company would fight like hell, given the proofs in the case, before they paid a dime.

The initial report was that Harry Conway was an asshole, a conclusion everybody, including the jury, had already come to.  He had been married and divorced four times with no children that anybody knew of.  Divorce judgments had been quick and dirty, and in all of them the women had walked away with nothing.  At least they got to walk away.  In the meantime, AAA Excavation was making a ridiculous amount of money on the shoulders of poorly paid laborers, with little capital expenditures, and only the significant salaries of the five foremen to account for its day to day overhead.  The company owned some machinery that had been paid for in cash.  A local bank held the payroll account as well as a revolving line of credit that hadn't been tapped in months.  AAA

Excavation was a cash cow, but the money was nowhere to be found. Company computers seized by court order were of no help.

Harry Conway lived alone east of Albuquerque in a secluded house protected by a gate. He drove an ancient pickup truck that sported a BushCheney bumper sticker. Displays of wealth, at least to the outside world, were nonexistent. Surveillance established that he kept pretty much to himself except for when he was at work. It also established that during the time he was being watched he never once visited a job site, apparently leaving that work to his henchmen. Once or sometimes twice a week in the early evening, a taxi would appear at the gate which would open to let it in. Inside was always a lone woman, always a different one, sitting in the back seat. She would spend the night. The next morning around 7, an empty taxi would arrive at the gate, be let in, and emerge a few minutes later with the woman in the back seat.

The long and short of the early investigation was that AAA Excavation and Harry Conway had a lot of money but no one had any idea where it was.

Will kept the Ruiz family up to date on the status of the appeal and the status of the investigation. Initially, he met with Rosie and Jorge but, after a few weeks, Jorge began to come to the office alone. He told Will that he thought his mom was decompensating as time went on. She still had her job at Garcia's, but she had lost weight and looked tired and ill. Her son thought that her grief over losing Felipe so soon after they had found happiness together had robbed her of any sense of purpose in life. They talked about grief counseling or a psychologist or antidepressants, and Jorge had discussed all of those with her but she would have none of it. She had stopped coming to Will's office because she couldn't stand to think of Harry Conway or "Arkansas Slim" Baker or any of it.

Yolanda accompanied Jorge on one of the visits and confirmed that her mother seemed to be spiraling ever deeper into depression.

Will had held off making any overtures about possible settlement to the new firm representing AAA Excavation in the appeal because he didn't want the defense to get the idea that the Ruiz family was desperate.  On the other hand, they were.

One afternoon, in the late fall after the verdict, Will picked up the phone and called lead counsel for AAA.  He had not known the lawyer during his years in Albuquerque but his colleagues and Alex all spoke highly of him.

"Emmett?  Will Bennett.  I wanted to talk to you about the Ruiz case."

"Will, that is amazing.  Just got off a conference call this morning with the bond company and the liability carrier and they wanted me to approach you about what it would take to get this one done."  Emmett Meyer went through the usual litany of the defenses they had, the state of the law, the very real possibility the verdict would be reversed, and the fact that the carrier had an exclusion for punitive damages.  But then he stopped and said something so unexpected that it took Will completely by surprise.

"So now I've gotten all the obligatory bullshit out of the way, here's what's really happening.  I represent one of the worst companies and worst human beings I have ever represented, and the carrier is scared to death that we are going to make some very bad law in New Mexico by extending the Delgato doctrine and, more importantly, exposing insurance carriers to huge verdicts.  Bottom line, I think, is that the bond company and the liability carrier together can put together a chunk of change to get this done.  Biggest problem is what the insurance company will do with the punies.  I'm looking to you to give us a demand that recognizes all of the above and I'll see what I can do.

Will hung up the phone.  Yowser.

In the same weeks that Will was reconnecting with his cases and following the AAA Excavation saga, he and Alex continued to see each other. Morton's in-laws had returned from Europe but were incredibly gracious about letting Will stay in the carriage house. He offered to pay them rent and was refused with the simple message that they knew how much Morton and Socorro thought of him and that was good enough for them. They asked no questions and left him to himself.

Truth be told, more nights than not he was staying at the townhouse with Alex. Most nights they were content to stay in with the cats but, as time went on, they ventured out to favorite restaurants, movies, and to listen to some music. At first, they both were hyper-paranoid about who they might run into but that too began to pass. The sexual part of it was the hardest to get back. Will struggled with visual images that made him a little crazy, but he kept reminding himself that it was only "body parts" and after a while had to admit to himself that he really was being a hypocritical asshole. Without even being told. So one night, he simply said 'screw it' and from then on, it was as though a light had gone off. No one would ever describe Alex Kennedy as being particularly patient but, on this issue, she had bided her time and was rewarded when that part of the nightmare was finally over.

In mid October, Alex and Will attended an Albuquerque Bar Association dinner that, for them, was like a coming out party, even though it was no secret in the legal community that they were an item again. Alex dressed to the nines and Will looked as good as he could. They took a collective deep breath and walked into the large dining room. Later, neither would say that they had a great time, but it was bearable. Members of the Johnston & Blackwell firm were quick to circle the wagons around them during the cocktail hour and at the dinner table. After dinner they danced together and whispered to each other: "If they can't take a joke…" And when the evening was finally over, they went back to the townhouse, poured an Irish, and headed for the hot tub.

That weekend Will moved back in permanently. They promised to pay attention to each other no matter what life dealt them, and while each was aware that a promise was only as good as the minute in which it was said, they each knew how close they had come to throwing away a very special thing.

# CHAPTER EIGHTEEN
## JACKIE

Jackie LaPointe had been a loner her entire life.  Deserted by her parents, she had been raised in a series of dirty, dreary foster homes.  She quickly grew too old to be attractive to prospective adoptive parents, and too angry for foster parents to hold onto for long.  She had gone to a series of high schools depending on where she was living and, at each one, quickly became an outlier with no friends and no social life whatsoever.  But she was brilliant far beyond normal, and when the SATs came around she scored in the genius range.  She applied to only local community colleges, was accepted into all of them, and chose a small one in northern Virginia.  She decided to major in law enforcement, and early on was rewarded with an internship with the Alexandria Police Department in its IT department.  After graduation she was offered a permanent job.

In college, Jackie distinguished herself both by holding a 4.0 GPA and by getting more and more Gothic tattoos and piercings.  She stayed a loner, lived by herself in the dorm all four years, and never so much as had a date.  From her perspective, the past was the past and she had no interest in reaching out to any of the foster families who had at least temporarily given her shelter.  Her view?  They got paid handsomely for offering her very little other than the basic necessities.

That upbringing made Jackie LaPointe very tough, emotionally bereft, and resilient.  She was also gay and had known it forever.

So she lived her life after college in a kitchenette apartment near the police department, spent her time learning computers and the IT business, and saving money for what she wasn't sure.

Along the way, she got to know a detective with the police department named Robert Davison and she allowed herself to open up just a bit to him.  He was a good cop, and when she was working cases with him it was the best time for her.  And she had met Will Bennett and Alex Kennedy who were working with

Robert trying to figure out who had killed Will's best friend and his best friend's wife.  For whatever reason, maybe because Robert seemed to like Will, she likewise developed, in her own way, an affection for both Will and Alex.

She knew the couple now lived in Albuquerque and, after the case was finished and Will had survived being shot, she thought about moving west.  There was nothing in northern Virginia other than memories she wanted to avoid.  She liked the outdoors, and she had heard that New Mexico and Albuquerque in particular were very accepting and open to all people, even gay young women who were tattooed and pierced.

The day after giving her notice to the police department and leaving a note of gratitude for Robert, she packed her vintage car with all of her belongings, which didn't even fill the car, and headed west.  Her original plan had been to get to Albuquerque and find an apartment, get settled, and then maybe call Alex and Will to see if they could help with a job search.  So of course she figured out where they lived as soon as she hit Albuquerque and knocked on their door.  And of course, because they were who they were, they invited her to stay with them for a while.  Both of them remembered Jackie and it took no time for Will to convince his new firm that they needed to hire her as a "gopher" who quickly morphed into their IT person who quickly morphed into their office manager.

Jackie had always thought that law school might be something to think about and, on a whim, took the LSATs, once again scoring in the highest percentage possible.  The University of New Mexico fell all over itself giving Jackie money to go there, and she decided that staying with Johnston & Blackwell and attending law school at UNM was a good path to take.  She took it.  And she began to think that if she were serious about being a lawyer she ought to lose at least the most obvious tattoos, so she began that process as money became available.

Jackie had finally found a home at Johnston & Blackwell working with people who genuinely cared about her and who she cared about.  Will and Alex remained her favorites, but she became close friends with Will's assistant, Liz LaRue, and others at the firm.  She even began to socialize some after work.

Then lightning struck.  Jackie was at the local Starbucks one morning treating herself to a latte when a young woman in front of her at the register dropped her purse on the floor, sending bills and coins flying everywhere.  Both knelt to pick it up, the woman said, "I'm so sorry," and then looked up at Jackie and their eyes met.  While their gaze couldn't have lasted more than a few seconds, it was as though time had stopped.  Later Jackie would relive that moment and remember it in exquisite detail.  She never forgot it.  When they got the money gathered and the young woman had paid for her drink, Jackie ordered, paid, and then to her immense shock asked, "I'm not in a great hurry, would you like to join me?"

To the young woman's own great shock, she replied, "Sure, that would be great."  They got their drinks and found a table.  The young woman's name was Josephine Lucas and she was a first year anesthesiology resident at UNM Hospital.  She, like Jackie, had grown up in the East but unlike Jackie had been raised in a very comfortable upper middle class family, had gone to undergrad at Boston College, and then medical school at Georgetown.  While her family had  wanted her to stay in the East, Josephine had just enough of an independent spirit to want to do something different and she had.  She was new in town, lived in an apartment near the hospital, and so far was immersed in the residency program.  As luck would have it on this particular morning she had no responsibilities and had decided to explore the downtown.  Jackie heard herself saying she likewise had no real pressing business at the firm and maybe they could take in some sights together.  Jackie called Liz and told her that she would be a little late that morning but that if anything came up to call her on her cell.  Liz would recall later that Jackie had sounded out of breath.  Which she was.  By noon Jackie LaPointe, for the first time in her life, was in love.

As the weeks went by, Jackie and Josephine saw each other when they could, which wasn't often given Josephine's schedule at the hospital and Jackie's first year in law school.  They were out one night having a rare dinner together when Josephine said out of the blue, "Why don't we move in together at my place?  Save money for both of us and we'd see more of each other."

"OK.  When?"

"This weekend soon enough?"

"Not really.  Tonight?"

"Perfect.  Let's stop by your place, get some of your stuff, and we'll get the rest this weekend."

That night Josephine and Jackie were together for the first time and, after that, almost never apart if they could help it.

Weeks and months went by and Jackie LaPointe had never been happier.  There had been difficult times at the firm when a crazy woman had killed three members of the firm before she herself was killed by Alex Kennedy.  After that there had been what seemed to be random killings at the courthouse that ended with Alex being kidnapped and then rescued.  Scary times, but they had survived and now Jackie had someone to share it with. She was number one in her class at UNM and still working full time at the firm, and Josephine was near the top of her residency class.  The biggest question for the two of them was what Josephine would do after her residency, whether she would stay in New Mexico or return back East closer to her family.  And then of course whether Jackie would stay in New Mexico with Johnston & Blackwell or follow Josephine back East if she went.  Hard stuff to think about.

One morning, shortly after the New Mexico Supreme Court ruled that same sex marriages were constitutional, Josephine asked Jackie to marry her.  That May, attended by the entire Lucas family and the entire firm of Johnston & Blackwell, the two were wed. Alex and Will stood in as Jackie's family.

But then Jackie's life turned upside down when Will Bennett announced abruptly that he was taking a leave of absence from the firm and going back to Michigan.  The news came out of the blue and stunned everybody.  Rosalind McManus would take over the day to day handling of the cases in the short term.  Both Jackie and Liz had tried to get information out of Will but he told them nothing and left as soon as he could saying that he would stay in touch.

It didn't take long for the rumor mill to get to Johnston & Blackwell on what had happened at the Judicial Conference some weeks back. It was just too juicy not to repeat. Again Jackie's world was rocked. She had thought Alex and Will, for a straight couple, had the very best marriage she had ever seen. Their relationship had been one of the bedrocks in Jackie's life. Now it seemed over.

As the weeks ground on, the Ruiz case was on track to go to trial if it survived the motion to dismiss, and Jackie was busy as anything getting it ready for Luis and Rosalind to try if it got that far. Then Luis got sick, Morton traveled to Michigan and returned with the news that Will would come back to help try the case. Jackie and Liz were beyond overjoyed.

After the trial, with Will deciding to stay in New Mexico, Jackie LaPointe went on a mission to do everything she could to punish Don Jenkins, the son of a bitch who had done so much to hurt the people she loved. She didn't know much about him other than he served on the District Court bench with Alex, and that long ago he had a relationship with her that had rekindled briefly at the judge's meeting. Jackie knew that Alex and Will were trying to work things out but she saw no reason why she shouldn't do something to Jenkins. She told no one, not even Josephine, about her plans.

Jackie read as much about Jenkins as she could find. A prosecutor for many years, he was described as very aggressive and successful, married with two kids, and appointed by the governor to the bench twenty years ago. Since that time he had served relatively quietly with little to make him stand out. She checked with some people she knew who described him as not very smart and very lazy but incredibly arrogant. As one person put it, "I can stand arrogance and I can stand ignorance but the combination of the two is more than I can take and Don Jenkins is both arrogant and stupid." His kids were grown and gone and his wife spent much of her time in Florida with her sisters. From afar, it didn't seem like much of a marriage and that made Jackie even angrier.

As soon as Jackie was convinced that the rumors about Jenkins and Alex were true, she began surveillance on him.  If she were candid, she would admit that she was stalking him, but whatever it was called, she was on it.  Fortunately, Josephine was working nights so Jackie could do a lot without anybody noticing.  As near as she could tell, Jenkins' wife was not in residence in their comfortable home near the campus.  Jackie's surveillance was haphazard at best for a number of reasons.  One, law school; two, her job; and three, Jenkins routinely left the courthouse around three in the afternoon which substantiated the lazy part.  As time wore on, Jackie discovered three very important things about Don Jenkins,  First, he was an amazing creature of habit, doing the same things on the same schedule almost without exception.  Two, every Saturday morning he would get on his mountain bike and ride the Bosque Trail next to the Rio Grande.  He would begin riding the trail promptly at 7:30 and be done no later than 9:30.  Third, almost every Tuesday, and for sure every Thursday, he would go home, change his clothes, don a dark haired wig and fake moustache and drive to East Central and troll for prostitutes.  Every Thursday, almost every Tuesday.  No wonder his wife spent so much time in Florida.  He would stop at the Starlight 66 Motel, one of the old Route 66 motels that had fallen on bad times, rent Room 231 every time, and then go searching up and down Central.  The arrogant piece of course was believing that a wig and fake moustache would help his anonymity even though every time he drove his own car with the vanity plate "Rule."

Jackie began to plot Will's Revenge.

# CHAPTER NINETEEN
## WILL'S REVENGE

On a Wednesday in late October, Jackie called the vice squad of the Albuquerque Police Department and left an anonymous message that a high ranking public official would be looking for a prostitute the following evening.  He would be driving a late model red Prius with the vanity license plate "Rule."  Once he made contact, he would drive the woman to Room 231 of the Starlight 66 Motel.  That Thursday, Jackie followed Jenkins home and then trailed him to the Starlight.  She placed another anonymous call to the *Albuquerque Tribune* and left a message that a high ranking public official would be picking up a prostitute on East Central and taking her  to Room 231 of the Starlight 66 Motel and that it might be a good idea to scramble together a camera crew.

She parked across the street at McDonald's and watched it all unfold.  First, she watched Jenkins leave the Starlight and drive down East Central.  Shortly afterward, two unmarked police cars pulled into the 7-Eleven lot just down from where she was parked and set up surveillance of the Starlight.  Shortly after that, another car pulled into the McDonald's, and a guy toting a camera with a very big lens and a tripod got out and set up aiming his camera at Room 231 across the way.  Not ten minutes later the red Prius drove into the Starlight parking lot and a man and woman emerged, climbed the stairs, and entered Room 231.  As soon as the door closed, six officers in plain clothes exited the unmarked cars, walked the stairs to the second floor of the motel, and staked out either side of the door with guns drawn.  In seconds, even from her vantage point across the street, Jackie heard, "POLICE.  OPEN UP!"  A moment later, she saw the woman open the door and let the police in.  She was also carrying a gun.  Within minutes, Don Jenkins, wig and moustache askew, was escorted out in handcuffs, taken across the street to one of the unmarked cars, and driven away with two of the police officers.  The woman and the other four officers climbed into the second unmarked car and also drove off.

Jackie watched the photographer snap a few more pictures, pack up, and take off.

She waited for a while longer and then left.

Chapter One of Will's Revenge was in the books.

The next morning, Jackie was up early and parked down the street from the Jenkins' house.  At about 8:30, she saw Jenkins drive out of his driveway in the red Prius.  At some point the night before he had apparently bonded out and gone back to get his car, probably figuring that a red Prius with a "Rule" license plate was best not seen in the parking lot of the Starlight 66 Motel in broad daylight.  Jackie followed him to the courthouse and then went to work.

On Saturday morning, Don Jenkins drove to the same parking lot he always drove to, parked the Prius, and unloaded his mountain bike.  About three miles out from where he parked, a beautiful stretch of the Bosque ran along a high rocky bluff with a beautiful view overlooking the Rio Grande and the west bank.  Just past the scenic view, the trail takes a sharp turn inland for a few hundred yards before correcting itself and leading back to the river. Jenkins paused briefly to take in the view, wondering what the next few days would bring after the arrest, when he felt a strong hand on his back that propelled him and his bicycle off the path and down the bluff to the river.  He had heard nothing and had seen nothing.

Unfortunately for the judge that section of the trail has a particularly steep grade and he and his bike rolled head over ass all the way to the bottom, landing in the tall weeds and mud next to the water.  He knew he was hurt, his shoulder ached and he felt blood coming down his face and on his arm and leg.  He lay still for a long time until he realized he was still connected to his bike by his clips.  He somehow wrenched out of them, found his cell phone, and called 911.

Taken by ambulance to the hospital, he spent the better part of the day in the emergency department.  Doctors stitched the lacerations on his face and arm, bandaged the leg, and placed his arm in a sling trying to hold the splintered pieces of his collarbone in place.  The ER doctor wasn't sure whether or not Jenkins would need surgery to put a plate on the collarbone and left that to the orthopedic surgeon who couldn't see him until Monday.  In the meantime, he was sent home with a lot of pain medication.  In the hours that followed, he took the medication very freely combining it with a generous amount of Stoli vodka straight.  It had not been a good week.  Somewhere between the drugs kicking in and the third glass of vodka, he wondered vaguely who had pushed him and why.  He would never know.

Chapter two of Will's Revenge was in the books.

Don Jenkins remembered almost nothing of Sunday. Monday morning he cleaned himself up as best he could and went to work with enough pain killers on board to stop a horse.  His appointment with the orthopedic surgeon wasn't until 2:00.  He sleepwalked through the morning, sighed with relief when he saw that the newspaper hadn't yet tumbled to his arrest by the undercover policewoman last Thursday, called his wife in Florida, and told her he'd had a minor accident on his bike.  He accepted sympathy from his staff and lawyers the rest of the morning.

Jenkins went to his appointment with the surgeon who took one look at the X-ray and informed the judge that he would need surgery that he was scheduling for the coming Thursday.  A plate with some small screws, immobilized for a few weeks, and hopefully a full recovery.

The judge returned home after the doctor's appointment, took the rest of the pain meds and quickly guzzled some more vodka.  His last waking thought before falling asleep at 6:00 was that it looked like the arrest was behind him and, with the surgery, he'd be good as new.  Lucky, very lucky, he told himself.

The next morning at 6:00 AM, Jenkins was awakened by a telephone call from a reporter from Channel 7 who asked him to comment on the story that was running that morning in the *Albuquerque Tribune* that he had been picked up for soliciting prostitution from an undercover policewoman.  The reporter was kind enough to inform him that the front page showed a picture of him being led out of Room 231 of the Starlight 66 Motel in handcuffs and a second picture that showed a Prius in the Starlight parking lot with the vanity plate "Rule" on it. Jenkins hung up on the reporter without saying a word, struggled downstairs, opened the door, and picked up the *Tribune* on his doorstep. The Channel 7 reporter had it right.

Chapter three of Will's Revenge was in the books.

The first Will and Alex heard of any of it was Tuesday morning when they went to Garcia's for breakfast and, walking in, Will saw the headline on the paper in the newspaper machine. He bought the paper, followed Alex into the restaurant scanning the front page, and gave it to her without saying anything. After they had both read the article, they looked at each other with a myriad of thoughts going through their minds. Will wished it wasn't so, but his primary emotion was one of glee, of revenge best served cold. Alex's train of thought was a bit more complicated as in, 'What the fuck was I thinking being with that asshole for one minute?' and more importantly 'What the fuck do I do with this asshole as Chief Judge of the district who also happens to be a former lover?'

She looked at Will and he looked back and then he couldn't contain himself. He smiled.

"Oh nice, Will. That's very helpful."

The story had detailed an anonymous tip the paper had received last Thursday and the decision to send a photographer to the motel. It also quoted from the police report that the man had invited the policewoman to the room, had given her money, and then had been placed under arrest. There had been a scuffle with the police woman that hadn't ended well for the "John" and had dislodged both his wig and his moustache. She had opened the door for the rest of the officers who had taken the "John" to the station to be booked. He was identified as Donald A. Jenkins, Second Judicial District Court Judge. He was booked and bonded himself out about 3:00 in the morning. The police had also indicated they were operating on an anonymous call they had received from a pay phone last Wednesday and, based on that call, had orchestrated the sting.  Neither the paper nor the police knew the identity of the caller.

"Whoever did it sure had it in for the judge."

"Hey, I have an alibi.  I was with you and Morton and Socorro Thursday night.  It wasn't me," he said with some level of happy indignation.

"Not saying it was, Will.  Just saying.  Somebody with a real bone to pick."  She left it at that.

"Think he'll resign?  Be the honorable thing to do."

"Then of course he won't do it.  Question is what do I do with it?"

Will thought for a minute but the answer was clear to both of them.  "Unless he voluntarily resigns, you have to punt this as soon as you can to Judicial Standards.  Anybody asks why, tell them.  Got to handle this straight up, sugar."

"I know you're right."  She paused.  "Sort of delicious isn't it?"

"Sort of."

"Will, you sure you were with me Thursday night?"

"'Bout to ask you the same thing."

"Wonder who it was?"

"Probably never know."

And they never would.  Nor would they ever know who it was on the Bosque Trail last Saturday morning whose hand propelled the good judge down the rocky cliff.

## CHAPTER TWENTY
## THE HONORABLE ALEXANDRA KENNEDY
## CHIEF JUDGE, SECOND JUDICIAL DISTRICT COURT

Alex Kennedy arrived at her chambers using the basement parking lot and up the back elevator.  As she drove down Lomas, she saw all the TV trucks outside the courthouse and was pretty sure they were all there to talk to somebody about Judge Donald Jenkins.

Karen Stillson was sitting at her desk.  "Jenkins is in your office, Judge.  I wasn't sure where else to put him."

Alex nodded and walked in.  Her first take was shock at his appearance.  She had missed the biking accident so the bandage on his face and the arm in a sling were all new to her.

"The police do this?"

"Biking accident Saturday.  No connection.  Surgery Thursday."

She really wanted to feel something for this guy. She really did.  They had meant something to each other a very long time ago and that should have been worth something.  But everything she had been through, everything Will had gone through, all the crap that had gone on was too much of an overload to feel anything.  So she sat quietly waiting for him to say something like 'I can explain' or 'it wasn't me.'  But he said nothing for a long time.

Finally.  "What do you think I ought to do, Alex?"

"Honestly, Judge, if I were you, I'd lawyer up as soon as I could.  You're gonna need help with the soliciting thing and you're gonna need a whole world of help with the Judicial Standards Commission.  I'm not touching this with a ten foot pole and you know why."

"But Alex, you could help, you really could.  Please? Coming from you, it would mean everything."

She wondered whether he meant the soliciting charge or the judicial review.  Or both.  But neither was her answer.

"Please leave the office, Judge.  You got yourself into this and you've got nobody to blame but yourself.  Now leave."

Jenkins started to say something more but caught himself. He rose painfully and left without a word.

Alex took a minute to breathe deeply and immediately dictated a memo about everything that had been said in her meeting with Jenkins.  She then sent an email to Judicial Standards asking them to take jurisdiction over whatever investigation would have to take place to determine whether Judge Jenkins would be removed from the bench if he didn't resign.  The immediate reply was that the investigation was already underway.

She took another deep breath, called Karen into her office, and asked what was on the docket for the day.  Back to normalcy.

## CHAPTER TWENTY-ONE
## ONE DOWN

On a Tuesday night in early October, a taxi drove up to Harry Conway's gated house.  The gate opened and the taxi drove in and up the drive.  A few minutes later, the taxi returned down the driveway, through the gate, and on its way in the direction of Albuquerque.  Fifteen minutes later, a black Ford F-150 pickup truck with a BushCheney bumper sticker drove down the driveway and headed north, its destination a barren, desolate piece of land just west of the foothills that led to the Sandias.  Three minutes into the trip, the truck slowed down long enough to pick up an individual in dark clothes and a ski mask.

Harry Conway woke up completely naked and spread eagled on the cold hard ground.  He looked up and down and realized he was tied to four stakes that had been pounded into the ground.  It was a dark moonless night but he saw two figures in black on their heels waiting for him to wake up.  He tried to remember what had happened.

The hooker had arrived on time in the taxi.  This was the third time for this one which was a record for him.  She was a little old for his taste and there was a sadness in her eyes, but nobody had ever accused Harry Conway of being overly sensitive when it came to feelings and he thought nothing of it.  Plus, she knew things and did things that made him forget her age or anything else for that matter.  He had her make them both a drink and made small talk while she walked around the place.  About the time he said something clever like 'let's see what you got' the room began to spin.  He grabbed a table to steady himself, wondered briefly if she had drugged him, and then fell unconscious at the woman's feet.  She walked into the next room, put on latex gloves she took from her oversized purse, opened a control panel and switched "Gate Camera" to "Off."  She then dragged Conway to the garage and lifted him into the bed of the pickup.  Conway wasn't light by any stretch of the imagination but the woman who was relatively small was possessed.  As she figured, the keys were in the truck.

She opened the garage door, backed out, down and out of the driveway, stopped to pick up the passenger down the road, and then drove in silence to what would be Harry Conway's killing ground. When they got him there, they got him out of the truck, stripped him, and staked him to the ground. The woman changed into all black clothes and donned a ski mask to match her partner. They waited for him to wake up.

Conway tried to scream and then for the first time realized there was duct tape across his mouth. A male voice from above him spoke softly and Conway noticed the odd shape of the knife he was holding.

"Mr. Conway, you are going to die tonight but you have a choice on how. Tell us where the money is hidden and you will die quickly. If you do not tell us, we will spend the next several hours cutting off pieces of your body until there is nothing left but your torso and most, but not all, of your head. Which is it?"

Conway looked at the mad man standing over him and shook his head violently. The other figure stepped up with what looked like wire cutters, bent over and cut off Harry Conway's index finger on his right hand. He screamed into the duct tape. The other index finger was next and now Conway's head was bobbing up and down. The man removed the duct tape and Conway told him where the house safe was but refused to tell him the combination. New duct tape was placed over Conway's mouth but before another finger came off, he was bobbing his head again. This time the combination. For a brief moment, Conway thought maybe they would spare him at least to find out if he was telling the truth but that didn't seem to make a difference to the two.

"I lied, Mr. Conway. You're not going to die quickly."

And he didn't. The pair was true to their word. It did take a long time and when they left, Harry Conway was no longer staked to the ground. He was blind because they had plucked both his eyes out and they had cut off both of his ears, his tongue had been replaced by his penis and testicles, and his hands and feet had been placed on his torso. He knew he was bleeding out as he heard them walk away, heard doors open, an engine start, and a vehicle pull away.  It was silent for a few moments and then Conway, barely on the edge of consciousness, heard from the holes where his ears had been, and then sensed, animals closing in on him.  His last thought was one more stab of pain when he felt teeth tearing into his torso.

The Ford F-150 retraced its path back to Conway's house, the passenger was dropped off where he had been picked up, and the truck continued on.  It entered the gate, parked in the garage with the keys carefully left in the ignition where they had been found.  The hooker went into the home office, put the gloves on, opened the control panel, and switched the "Gate Camera" to "On."  She moved to the picture behind the desk, removed it, and found the safe.  Conway had told the truth about the combination and she filled two garbage bags with money.  She spent the next hour making certain that she had left no trace of herself or the pills she had put in Conway's drink.

At exactly 7:00 the next morning, the same taxi pulled up, the gate was opened, and several minutes later, the taxi came down the driveway, through the gate, and headed towards Albuquerque.

Over the next week to ten days, Will Bennett continued to negotiate with Emmett Meyer, who was still handling the appeal, without getting much of anywhere. They both agreed to use former Judge Sitterly as a mediator to see if she could talk sense into one of them.

On a bright early November Monday morning, they met in Judge Sitterly's private office. Rosie and Jorge were there with Will and Rosalind, and Meyer was there with representatives of both the liability carrier from Philadelphia and the bond company from Boston. Will and Rosalind were both shocked at Rosie's condition. She had lost a lot of weight, her hair was greasy and stringy, and her skin had a pasty pallor that looked awful. At an early break, Will got Jorge aside in the men's room and asked whether his mom was sick.

"Nothing physical, amigo, just sick at heart. Doesn't eat, doesn't care what she looks like, moves like a robot one foot in front of the other. Yolanda and I got her to some grief counseling but it sure doesn't seem to be helping. Be good if we could get closure on this, Will."

And at about 7:00 that evening, they did. After spending most of the day complaining about the verdict, the injustice of it all, the state of the law in New Mexico, and the amount of the punitive damages for which it turned out there was full insurance coverage, the two carriers agreed to pay a total of thirteen million dollars to the Estate of Felipe Ruiz to settle the case against AAA Excavation. The carriers tried to insist on a confidentiality clause because several other former employees were making noises of making the same sorts of claims. Felipe Ruiz had paid the ultimate price but there were three other fatalities and dozens of injuries that were still on the sidelines. Rosie Ruiz would not agree to a settlement with a confidentiality clause and it was finally taken off the table by the defense.

Will and Rosalind both hugged Rosie and both could feel her bones through her clothes.  Will had a fleeting thought that he hoped she would live long enough to enjoy some of what the money could buy.  Jorge talked about setting up annuities for all of them, and Rosie and Jorge talked about a foundation in Felipe's name that they could use to help people in need.  They all agreed to reconvene within the week to talk about the future and what the money could do for them and for others.

After Rosie and Jorge left, Rosalind and Will met up with Liz and Jackie at the Coppertop to celebrate.  They ordered a bottle of the best champagne that the 'Top had, which frankly wasn't going to break the bank, filled their glasses, and Will said simply, "To the Team."

"To the Team," they all said raising their glasses.

Four different cabs got them all home safely.

Will carefully opened the door to the townhouse as quietly as he could. He staggered out of all of his clothes in the living room and then got on his hands and knees and crawled up the stairs congratulating himself on how stealthy he was.  At the top of the stairs, he was met with two feet and ankles on the landing.  "Uh oh, I'd know those finely turned ankles anywhere," he thought vaguely. Summoning what energy he had left and with as much dignity as he could manage, which was a bit difficult given he was naked, he grabbed the hand rail and pulled himself into a standing, or at least semi-crouching position.

"Hi honey, I'm home."

"I gather you settled."

# CHAPTER TWENTY-THREE
## MARGARET ESPINOZA

The next morning came way too early for Will, helped in no small way by Alex making as much noise as she could getting ready for work and whistling while she did. It became abundantly clear to Will that sleeping in was not an option so he made it to the bathroom, started with two Tylenol, and then surveyed the damage in the mirror. It wasn't pretty. 'How do bags like that just grow overnight' he wondered as he prepared for what he hoped would be a miracle shower.

Alex breezed into the bathroom with a mug of coffee.

"Here…honey. Have a wonderful day." Blew him a kiss, smiled, and she was gone. Will took a big sip of the coffee and immediately regretted it. He should know better than to ever trust his wife when it came to making coffee. This time it should have been served with a fork and a steak knife. He poured out a little and replaced it with some water. It became at least drinkable.

While in the shower, he mused over yesterday's events and the settlement for Rosie and her family. He had been surprised when the carriers had blown through the compensatory damages and began to talk in between compensatory and punitive damages as a settlement range. Will was still amazed at the difference between the law in the State of Michigan, where tort reform was king, and New Mexico where defendants and their insurers feared to tread if they could possibly avoid it. He was sure that Judge Sitterly had been pretty forthcoming talking about the law in New Mexico and was also pretty sure that Emmett Meyer had also helped. The settlement would take care of Rosie, Jorge and Yolanda for the rest of their lives and Johnston & Blackwell had had a pretty good day as well.

Showered, shaved, and dressed, he stopped at Garcia's for a big breakfast that he hoped would soak up some of the leftover alcohol and then went on to the office.

The only message when he got there was from Melony Vega, the receptionist, as Liz, Rosalind, and Jackie had yet to arrive.  It was urgent.  "Call Det. Espinoza ASAP" and gave the number.

'Oh, this can't be good' he thought as he made his way to his office.

Albuquerque Police Detective Margaret Espinoza was a good friend of Alex's who had done much over the past months to investigate the mayhem that had plagued Johnston & Blackwell as well as the Bernalillo County Courthouse.  She had been a single mom coming up through the ranks of the Albuquerque Police Department and, largely because of her work clearing up the murders at the courthouse, had become the darling of the local news media.  It had come with as big a price tag as a parent can pay.  Her only child, Ronnie, had been one of the victims of the murderer and Margaret's sole source of love and emotional support was gone forever.  Alex had spoken at Ronnie's service, and since then her friendship with Margaret had deepened to the point where the two were such good friends that Judge Kennedy recused herself from any cases in which Detective Espinoza was the lead investigating detective.

Will got a cup of coffee, went to his office, closed the door, and dialed the number.

"Will?"

"Margaret.  How are you?"

"Getting by. Thanks.  You?"  And the question mark meant she really was asking.

"Gettin' there.  Thanks."  The slightest of pauses and Margaret had her game voice on.

"Glad to hear it.  You have some time this morning?  I'd like to stop by and talk to you about something I'm working on with the Sheriff's Department."

Like you tell a homicide detective you didn't have time for her.  Like you'd tell a judge you'd get back to them.  Right.

"Morning is all free.  That work?"

"Perfect.  10:00 OK?"

Will looked at his watch.  9:15. He felt a vague rumbling somewhere below his stomach that reminded him of last night.

"Sure.  You coming here or do you want to meet somewhere?"  Will was acutely aware of how much time Detective Espinoza had spent at the law firm investigating the murders that had taken place and thought she might want to meet at a neutral site.  No such luck.

"Be there at 10:00.  See you then."  The phone went dead.


Will got up to get another cup of coffee and ran into Liz in the break room.  Whoa.

"You OK?"

"Look at me.  Whadda you think?  Jesus, Will, I'm gettin' too old for this shit."

Just as Will was about to make some supportive comment like 'you've never looked better,' Jackie walked in and, if possible, made Liz look almost normal.

"We need to think about hourly work, guys.  This contingency stuff can kill you."  She damn near pushed both Will and Liz aside to get to the coffee.

Rosalind was next and pissed the other three off.  Well coifed, well dressed, well made up, she bounced in as though she had had twelve hours of sleep and a massage.  Maybe even sex.

"HEY.  HOW IS EVERYBODY TODAY?  WHAT A BLAST LAST NIGHT, RIGHT?"

Jackie looked at Will and Liz and rolled her eyes.

"Rosalind.  Use your indoor voice.  In fact, use your library voice, OK?"

Rosalind studied the three of them, acknowledged their pain with a nod of her head, poured her coffee, and retreated to her office.

"I'm going to kill her," they said almost in unison.

On the intercom, Will heard himself being paged.

"Mr. Bennett, please call the receptionist."

He looked at his watch.  10:00.  Why did he have a premonition of doom?

He soon found out.

Will was startled by Margaret Espinoza's appearance.  He hadn't seen her since he had gone to Michigan and she looked as though she had aged twenty years.  Her hair was unkempt and unwashed and she had lines in her face that hadn't been there even a few months before.  She was much thinner than he had remembered and her clothes, which were always stylish and trim, were now wrinkled and messy.  She was not there to make small talk.

Without even a 'glad to have you back,' she started in.

"Will.  Let me get to the point.  Three days ago, hikers in the area just at the foothills of the Sandias came across the remains of something.  They weren't even sure if it was human or animal remains, they called 911 and a Bernalillo County Sheriff's Deputy responded.  I'm told his first response was to recognize it was human and his second was to throw up all over himself. Reinforcements and the crime lab people were called and the area cordoned off."  She looked at her notes and went on and Will wondered what the hell this had to do with him but his premonition of doom deepened.  "It was a badly decomposed, badly eaten, white male who had been there for some days and who had provided protein for any number of beings in the area from coyotes to vultures.  He had also been the subject of a lot of serious mutilation, as in removal of body parts."  Notes again.  "Medical examiner pegs time of death at a week ago, but hedges it by saying there was so little left it's at best an educated guess.  They got what was left into body bags, apparently it took more than one or two, and got it to the morgue.  Someone or something had eaten the bejesus out of the face and even dental imprints were hard to come by."  Another pause, this one more for effect than real. "Preliminarily, the pathologists are thinking the remains are Harry Conway.  Which is why I'm here."


Will Bennett kept his game face on but had the vaguest of feelings that something relatively big was alive and wandering in his intestines.  It was not the greatest of mornings to have been way overserved the night before.

"AAA Excavation."

"Exactly.  You just hit them for some ridiculous verdict in the millions of dollars, the feds and the state are undertaking a corruption investigation, I'm told you just settled with the insurance companies for millions, and what we think is what's left of Harry Conway is dead in the high desert."

"Am I a suspect?"  Will thought that to be extraordinarily funny.  But Detective Espinoza didn't.  Will had a fleeting memory of a T shirt that said 'Remember, the police don't think it's near as funny as you.'

"Not yet.  But I'm not crossing you off the list either." Was that an attempt at humor?  He didn't know but voted for the worst wondering where he had been a week ago and if he had an alibi.

She went on.  "The sheriff's deputies went through Conway's house and other than he wasn't there and they couldn't find him, everything seemed in order.  Except one thing.  There is a surveillance camera at the gate of his house and on October 7th from a little after seven in the evening to a little after two in the morning, the tape was blank.  Somebody intentionally turned it off. Last thing we see is a taxi with a woman in the back seat arriving right around 7:00 and the next thing is shortly after 2:00 when it comes back on.  Around 7:00 AM, the same taxi is at the gate and shortly after that leaves with what we think is the same woman in the back seat."

"Able to identify either the taxi or the woman?"

"Here's what's strange. Other than the car is yellow, there are no identifying characteristics. It's an old Chevy Impala. With no license plate. Same car in the morning. We've checked with all the cab companies and they all say it's not theirs."

She looked at her notes again. "Conway's house is swept way clean, as in too clean, as in somebody took a lot of time to sweep and clean. Thoughts?"

He thought for a moment. He knew why she had come to see him. If anybody had a reason to kill Harry Conway, it was Rosie Ruiz.

"What brings you here, Margaret?"

"As near as we can tell, anybody who has ever met Harry Conway even for the briefest moment hates him enough to kill him. It would include anybody who ever worked for him. It would include his ex-wives." She took a breath. "And it would include Ms. Ruiz. The sheriff has ultimate jurisdiction over the case but asked me to help, I guess in large part because she knows I know you and Alex. I wanted to do you the courtesy of telling you all this instead of just barging in on Ms. Ruiz." She paused again. "My spies tell me you may be back for good, Will. That's a good thing."

"I know, Margaret. Thanks. Want me to set up a meeting with you and Rosie?"

"As soon as possible, Will."

"I'll call her and get her work schedule and get back to you in an hour or so. That work?"

"Yep."

She got up to leave.

"Margaret?" She turned back to him. "How are you doing?"

There was the slightest of smiles. "'Bout like I look, Will. 'Bout like I look. But thanks for asking." Detective Margaret Espinoza drew herself up and left without another word.

The first thing Will did was call his spouse who fortunately was in chambers.

"Jesus, Alex. Margaret was just here and I almost didn't recognize her. She looks terrible."

Alex had forgotten that Will hadn't seen her since he'd been back and somehow her name hadn't come up in conversation.

"I know. It's awful. I keep trying to get her to go to grief counseling or see a shrink or get on antidepressants, but so far she's resistant to anything. Almost as though she's doing some sort of penance for what happened to Ronnie. It's awful." Then it dawned on Alex that the conversation had started with 'Margaret was just here…'

"Will, why was Margaret seeing you?"

"Apparently Harry Conway went wandering in the desert a few nights ago and came upon a very unfortunate end. Make that very, very unfortunate. Margaret got asked by the sheriff to run down Rosie Ruiz as the possible killer and she was kind enough to stop here to set up the meeting as opposed to pounding on Rosie's door."

"Rosie Ruiz killing Harry Conway? I can't imagine her doing something like that even if she were strong enough. Can you?"

"No way. But I'm thinking maybe she should lawyer up. Whadda you think?"

Alex thought for a moment. The thought that Rosie would do anything so violent was unimaginable but she had been through so much so who really knows.

"Couldn't hurt, I guess. Not like she doesn't have the money now."

"True. Rita?" Rita Alvarson was a longtime friend of Alex's and was widely considered to be the number one criminal defense lawyer in the state.

"Who else?"

"I'll call her. Thanks. See you regular time?"

“Yup.  Love you, Will.”
“Me too you.”

Two days later Margaret Espinoza, Rosie Ruiz, Rita Alvarson, and Will met in the conference room at Johnston & Blackwell.  The day before Rita, Rosie, and Will had met at length.

Rosie didn't look any better than she had, even with the settlement behind her and the financial resources to do pretty much anything she wanted to do.  When Will told her about Harry Conway dying, she showed no emotion whatsoever.  Just the blank stare he had gotten used to.  Will decided not to go into details of what had been left of Mr. Conway and hoped Margaret Espinoza would have the decency also to avoid it.  The possible time of death had been narrowed down to a 48 hour period.  On both days, Rosie had worked a full shift at Garcia's and had gone straight home, gotten something to eat, and then had gone right to bed.  Will called Jorge who confirmed that when he got home from work around 8:00 each evening, his mother was already in bed.  He thought that Yolanda would also confirm that her mother had been home on both nights as well.

The meeting with Detective Espinoza was remarkably uneventful.  She asked Rosie about her whereabouts and got the same information that Rita and Will had gotten the day before.  Will volunteered that both her kids had been home and would vouch for their mom if necessary.  Almost perfunctorily, the detective said that if it became necessary, she would get in touch with Will but at this point she didn't think she would need it.

"I told the sheriff I would follow up with you and I have.  Can't imagine it will have to go any farther than this."

She got up to leave, said her goodbyes and started to walk out the door, but turned back.

"Ms. Ruiz, can you think of anybody who might have done this?"

And only because he had come to know Rosie Ruiz so well did Will notice there was the briefest change in her eyes.  Just for an instant but it startled him to see it.  What was it?  Fear?  Some secret knowledge?  He didn't know but it was something.

Fortunately, he didn't think anybody else noticed it or if they did, it passed.

"No, Detective.  I know nobody who would kill Harry Conway."

The detective looked at her for a heartbeat too long.  Had she seen the change in Rosie's eyes?

"All right.  Thank you.  If I need anything more, I'll go through either Rita or Will.  I'm sorry for your loss, Ms. Ruiz." And she meant it.

"Thank you."

The meeting was over and Will could feel himself let a rush of air out.  How did people do criminal defense for a living?  Rita Alvarson was pleased with the way things had gone.  She and Detective Espinoza had a long history and both had a begrudging respect for the other.  Nevertheless, even Rita felt herself relax for the first time.

Will thought about Rosie's reaction to the question about who might have killed Conway but didn't quite know what to do with it.  While they exchanged pleasantries and she got ready to leave, Will decided to let it be.  He knew her well enough that if he called her on it, she would immediately close down.  So asking about it wasn't going to get him anywhere.

Rita indicated she needed to talk to Will about another matter and Rosie Ruiz left.

She turned to Will.  "She knows something, doesn't she?"

"Jesus, Rita.  Why do you say that?"

"I saw her eyes change when Margaret asked her that last question and I know you saw it too.  It wasn't much but it was something.  What worries me is if Margaret saw it too."

Will trusted Rita and, after all, she was working on the same side.

"I saw it and I don't know what to make of it.  Thought about asking her but she'd just shut down.  But yeah, it worries me."

"You think Jorge might have been involved?"

He thought about it for a minute.

"Jorge Herrera is a young man who, because of Felipe Ruiz, is going to make something of himself.  No doubt.  On the other hand, he loved Felipe like his own father.  If he had a father.  So being there and seeing what happened to his stepdad?  Does he have that kind of violence in him?  I don't know, Rita.  I truly don't."  He paused.  "But I'd sure understand if he did."

"I think we need to talk to him, Will.  I really do."

"Let me take a run at it first before we get you involved, OK?"

She had her doubts because when it came to criminal law, Will was clueless.  But she understood the why of it.

The next day Will and Jorge met after Jorge got off work.  They met at a local coffee shop, talked a little bit about the settlement, and then Will asked the question that had been on his mind for twenty-four hours.

"Jorge, look me straight on, look me right in the eyes, and tell me whether you had anything to do with Harry Conway's death."  Even as he said it, it sounded ridiculous like something out of a B movie or trash paper back.  Really, Will, 'look me straight on, look me right in the eyes?'  But it got Jorge's attention.  He looked at Will straight on for a long moment.

"Will, I wanted that motherfucker dead.  I'm glad he's dead.  I want "Arkansas Slim" Baker dead just as bad.  I think about it a lot and I've got the guts to do it.  You know that, don't you?"

Will nodded.

“But you know why I didn’t kill Conway and why I won’t kill Baker?”

Will shook his head.

“Felipe.  I owe him and his memory to make something of myself.  That’s what I promised him and I’m going to live up to it. Get it?”

Will nodded.

“But I’m glad he’s dead and I hope Baker is next.”

Will nodded.

“Any ideas on who did it, Jorge?”

“Could be anyone who ever worked for him, Will. Everything he touched was evil.”

“You know I have to ask these questions, don’t you?”

“Sure.  I get it.  But I’m telling you right now that my mom had nothing to do with it and Yolanda didn’t have anything to do with it and I didn’t have anything to do with it.  Hell, thanks to you, we’re millionaires.”

‘Yeah,’ Will thought to himself, ‘that’s true. But what a way to get there.  But Conway died before the mediation and before the settlement.  And no money can take away that kind of pain.  And “Arkansas Slim” is still alive. Wonder what he’s thinking about now?’

“I believe you, Jorge.  It needed to be asked.”

“Sure.”

They shook hands and parted.  On the way back to his office, Will could not get his mind off that instant when Rosie Ruiz’s eyes flashed.  Maybe nothing, maybe something.  But he believed his clients.  Idly, his mind wandered to “Arkansas Slim.”

# CHAPTER TWENTY-FIVE
## "ARKANSAS SLIM" BAKER

"Arkansas Slim" Baker was scared shitless.

Word had gotten around how Harry Conway had died.  One of the AAA Excavation lawyers had seen the initial sheriff's report and had called the five foremen together to tell them to watch their backs.  'Jesus, somebody cut his dick off and put it in his mouth.  Who would do that?'  The medical examiner had concluded that Conway had still been alive when the animals got to him but had died soon after.  How long he had been conscious while his body parts were being cut off was an unknown and always would be.  It had to have been a long time.

Baker was a bully and always had been.  He had grown up in rural Arkansas beaten daily by his father who was as mean a man as Baker had ever met.  When he wasn't beating Ralph (his real name), he was beating Ralph's mother, brothers, and sisters.  When he was old enough to understand, it was also clear to him that his father was having sex with Ralph's sisters.  Thankfully, his father was killed in a bar fight when Ralph was 17 but, by then, the die was cast.  He had dropped out of high school in the 10$^{th}$ grade and had gotten a job at the local feed store hauling 50 and 100 pound bags of grain and feed.  He was mean and tough, got himself into some petty stuff with the local sheriff, started calling himself "Arkansas Slim", and ended up enlisting in the U.S. Army in lieu of several months in the county jail.

In the purest of coincidences, he became a jailer at one of the military prisons in Iraq and was dishonorably discharged for the mistreatment of prisoners on his watch.  Fortunately, there were others in the prison who had had the incredible stupidity to take photographs of the abuse and it was those miscreants who the Army court martialed.  Baker was just discharged and sent home.  He kicked around for a while in the Southwest doing odd jobs until he fell into a job that perfectly fit both his personality disorder and his skill set.  AAA Excavation was looking for a crew foreman. Baker filled out an application, met for five minutes with Harry Conway, and was given the job to start the next day.

For Baker, it was livin' the dream.  He got paid a ridiculous amount of money to berate and sometimes beat other human beings, a skill he had developed in the Army prison.  Best of all, he rarely had to lift anything heavier than a night stick.

It was a perfect gig until that spic got killed in the cave in. Once the family got themselves a lawyer, Baker's life began to unravel at a rather furious pace.  There was the initial investigation by the state authorities, then his statement under oath got taken in the lawsuit, then he had to testify at trial and that apparently didn't go very well, then the state and federal investigations got serious, and Baker and the others lost their jobs.  He had saved some money from the wages he earned and decided to take some time off before looking for other work.

Then Harry Conway got himself killed and "Arkansas Slim" Baker was no longer king of the hill.  He and the others got together shortly after Conway was found and got stinking drunk trying to figure out what they were going to do.  AAA's lawyers had told them they might be criminally charged, but it was unlikely as the target was Conway himself.  But whether they were going to be charged or not, it was clear there were going to be lots of questions to answer as a part of the investigations.  The five crew chiefs had always wondered where Conway kept his money.  They knew there had to be plenty of it even with how much he paid them.  None of them had the guts to ask him so nobody knew.

That night, three of the five said they were leaving town and, even as drunk as they were, wouldn't tell each other where they were going.  Up to that night, Baker figured he'd stay in New Mexico, let things settle out, and then get new work, hopefully doing the same kind of thing he'd done for AAA.  Now he wasn't so sure.  What if Conway's death was related to the Ruiz death?  If it was, somebody would sure as hell be looking for him next.

That's what scared him shitless.

And it should have.


Ten days after what was left of Harry Conway was found in the desert north of Albuquerque, Dusty Crenshaw, one of the AAA crew chiefs, was stabbed to death as he was leaving a bar in the South Valley.  To the police it was a simple random robbery homicide like they had seen dozens of times before.  Crenshaw's wallet and an undisclosed amount of cash were missing.  The police interviewed the customers in the bar and, per usual, all of them had been in the men's room at the time Crenshaw left the bar and hadn't seen anything.  The owner of the bar, who was bartending that night, was a little more forthcoming as this was the third homicide in the last six months either in his bar or in the parking lot and he was a tad concerned that the city might shut him down.  He needn't have worried about it.  There were several other bars in the South Valley that had an even worse record and they were still open.  What nobody knew was that there was an unwritten policy in the Albuquerque Police Department that, after sunset, regular patrols steered clear of the Valley unless there was a specific 911 call.  No sense asking for trouble.

Nevertheless, the owner told the police that Crenshaw had been flashing a wad of money that would choke a horse and bragging to anyone who would listen that there was a lot more where it came from.  That was all the police needed to write it off as a random act of violence.  The investigation was cursory at best given how shorthanded the Homicide Division was.  It briefly crossed Margaret Espinoza's desk but neither the detective nor anybody else tumbled to the fact that both Conway and Crenshaw were connected to AAA Excavation.  When the police searched Crenshaw's apartment, they did find out one thing.  He had been telling the truth when he had boasted there was a lot more money where that had come from.  They found $50,000 in small bills in a bureau drawer.

Baker heard about Crenshaw's death in a telephone call from "Big" McCroskey, one of the remaining crew chiefs, who had seen it on the news.  Ralph hung up, walked into his bathroom, and threw up.  The next days he spent alone in his apartment, drinking vodka from the bottle, deeply paralyzed by the fear that threatened to choke him to death.  For the first time in his life, "Arkansas Slim" realized consciously what he should have known all along.  Like his father, and like all bullies, he was a coward and what was happening to him was, for lack of a better term, a "coming out."  The vodka only helped to get him to pass out and only lasted until he woke up.  Then he could get started again.  He knew he had to make a plan as soon as he sobered up.  Except he was never sober and that was a setback to planning for the future.  It was a serious mistake.

Two days later it got worse.  One of the other foremen, Terry Alright, had decided to move to Las Vegas, New Mexico, north of Santa Fe to get some distance from AAA Excavation, Harry Conway, and the investigations.  Like the other crew chiefs, he had money to burn and, like the others, wasn't smart enough to be quiet about it.  He rented a small furnished apartment in a shabbier part of town, paid cash for the deposit and first month's rent, and used an alias on the rental application.  Three days after he moved in, one of the other tenants noticed a foul smell coming from Apartment 3A and notified management.

What management found were the remains of Terry Alright, his throat slit from end to end.  His wallet and any other cash or valuables were missing.  It took a while before police found out it was really Mr. Alright as opposed to the alias on the rental application.  That went out over the usual law enforcement channels and when it did, it got to Margaret Espinoza who, almost randomly, began to put it together.  She had the Conway killing that the sheriff still had jurisdiction over, and now she was looking at a police report from the Las Vegas Police Department that identified an alias as Terry Alright, a former crew chief of AAA Excavation.  She retrieved the Dusty Crenshaw file and confirmed he had been one of the crew chiefs as well.

In the months since her son had died, Margaret Espinoza had simply been putting one foot ahead of the other, not really living at all, showing up at work and putting in her time, but little else.  She and Alex Kennedy had gotten even closer over the last months and Alex had pleaded with her to get out from under the cloud of her son's death.  But she wasn't ready.  So she had lived in grey.

Until now.  The connection of these deaths and several other homicides she was working on seemed to spark her back to life almost like a light bulb turning back on after a long time unlit.  She began to get back to who she was.  A cop.
She identified the three crew chiefs who were still alive: Buck Lewis, Big McCroskey, and Ralph Baker were still alive as far as she knew.  She ordered that patrol officers stop at last known addresses and advise the men what had happened.  There was still no real connection other than AAA but her instincts told her differently.  Too many coincidences.  For the first time since her son's death, she went out and got herself the biggest latte she could order, went back to her cubicle, put her feet up, and began to think about the connections.  She wasn't back all the way but the light was coming back on.

McCroskey called Baker to tell him about Alright but it went to voice mail because Ralph was passed out on the couch.  "Big" realized it was a bit harsh but he was busy packing to get out of town so he left a voice mail.  Within minutes of leaving the message, "Big" got a visit from the Albuquerque police telling him what he already knew.  He thanked the police profusely, closed and locked his door, and continued to pack.

Several hours later, Baker woke up enough to pee, listened to the message, and promptly threw up again, this time not making it all the way to the bathroom.  He also had not heard the police knock on his door.  What he should have done was what McCroskey was doing…packing and making a run for it.  But he didn't.  He uncapped his last bottle of vodka and got after it.  It was a second very big mistake.

The next day, "Arkansas Slim" discovered he indeed was out of both vodka and food, and although the food probably could have waited, the vodka couldn't.  It was a two block walk to the grocery and liquor store and he didn't trust himself to drive even that short a distance.  So he put on his shirt and jeans, got some of the cash from under his bed, and headed out.  He avoided everybody he could on the short walk just in case and stayed very close to the mostly empty storefronts in case he needed to rest for a minute.  His first stop was the grocery store for some frozen dinners and then he went to the liquor store and loaded up as many half gallons of Popov Vodka as he could carry.  They loved him at the liquor store.  One, he recently was buying ridiculous amounts of vodka, and two, he always paid in cash.  Loaded down with the necessary sustenance to keep him going for a few more days, he started back to his apartment trying to clear his mind enough to figure out what to do.  He knew he had to get out of Albuquerque but didn't have a clue about where to go.  He thought about Arkansas but that state held only the worst of memories for him.  Maybe California.  Yep, California.  That would work.

Baker vaguely noticed a woman coming towards him.  She had on one of those things they wrap around their heads and faces and, as she got closer, he muttered 'fuckin' Arabs' to himself.  As soon as they passed each other, she turned.  Baker felt what he thought was a hand on the small of his back that caught him off guard and pushed him into a recessed doorway.  The next thing he felt was a very sharp object that entered his back, went through his rib cage, and into his heart.  He felt the object being pulled out and as he fell, his vodka bottles broke on the sidewalk.  He fell into the glass and vodka as he felt himself dying.  He looked at the woman through clouding eyes.  She leaned over and whispered 'at least you've still got your dick, motherfucker.'  Then she whispered a name in his ear and left.  It was the last thing "Arkansas Slim" Baker would ever hear.

# CHAPTER TWENTY-SIX
## AFTERMATH

When Baker's death found its way to Detective Espinoza's desk, she became truly alarmed about the safety of the last two crew chiefs, "Big" McCroskey and Buck Lewis. Patrol officers were sent to their addresses but were advised by the landlords that both men had left their apartments and most of their belongings and furniture and had departed for parts unknown. She issued APBs for both of them to be stopped if they were still in New Mexico so that she could get them into protective custody until she got this sorted out. Plus she had some questions for them and was just as sure the federal and state investigators would as well. What she didn't know was that both of them were long gone, Lewis heading east and McCroskey west.

Margaret Espinoza had not become an Hispanic woman homicide detective without being very smart. Starting years before as a rookie cop on the beat, she had worked her way up, passing the detective exams one by one, working harder than her male peers, and until a few months ago, being a single mom. She laid out everything she knew about the four murders and, not for the first time, realized how precious little she had to work with. The Conway investigation by the sheriff's department had gotten nowhere. The taxi cab had never been located and the hooker was a mystery. They had found a number of prostitutes who had serviced Conway from time to time over the years but none of them had seen him in the weeks leading up to his death.

The Crenshaw murder could just as well have been a random robbery, especially if he had been bragging about all the money he was carrying. Terry Alright had rented his apartment under an alias, so whoever killed him, if there were a connection to AAA Excavation, would have had to have known who he was and where he was going and tracked him to Las Vegas. That likewise could just as easily have been a random robbery.

As to Baker, there were no witnesses and certainly no suspects.  It had taken a while to even have somebody show some interest in his body as most people walking by simply thought he was a drunk sleeping it off in the doorway, especially with the smell of vodka all over him.

She thought about Felipe Ruiz and wondered again if his death had anything to do with it.  She could see the connection if it were just Conway and Baker but why Alright and Crenshaw?  She truly didn't believe Rosie Ruiz had anything to do with it.  When she met with her, she recognized that look of emptiness because it was what stared back at her in the mirror ever since her son had died.  She had followed up on Jorge Herrera but had ruled him out simply because he worked too many hours and had the same alibi as his mother.  Unless they were in it together.  With Will and Rita Alvarson in tow, she interviewed Yolanda Herrera who confirmed that her  mother would get home from work, have something to eat, and then go right to bed, often times not even speaking to her children.  So even if the Ruiz death was a connection to the other murders, it wasn't his widow or her kids.

The one other thing that bothered her was that even though the case was helping get her back from her mourning for her son, she really didn't care about these four men.  By all accounts, all of them had been some of the worst examples of humanity, little better than slave owners and overseers.  In her own mind, Albuquerque was a better place without them in it.  Not exactly the right mind set for the lead detective to take, but there were plenty of other cases she was working on in which the victims deserved far more justice than these four.  She would continue to keep the case active and continue to pursue leads if and when they appeared, but it was no longer, if it ever had been, at the top of her list.

# CHAPTER TWENTY-SEVEN
## THE MONEY

Will and Alex both learned of the deaths of Crenshaw, Alright, and Baker but other than Baker's, which Will particularly took delight in, the news had little impact on them. They had gotten almost back to where they had been before the whole Jenkins affair. Will still had just the slightest doubts that would float across his mind from time to time but he kept them to himself. It would do no good to share them with Alex because she couldn't prove a negative. He thought about Robert and decided against it, thought about Rusty or Grace or maybe even seeing a psychologist, but chose not to do any of it. He figured time would heal and indeed it seemed to be working.

As for the Honorable Donald Jenkins, the New Mexico Judicial Standards Commission found him decidedly dishonorable. After its investigation, it established that he had been meeting with prostitutes for the entire time he was on the district court bench. What was worse for the entire bench was that several other judges were aware of his sexual proclivities and had simply turned the other way. The Chief Judge of the district had her hands full with the media for a number of days as they happily described the results of the leaked investigation and also happily interviewed any number of prostitutes who had been with Jenkins. It was not a story that was going to end well for the judge. And it didn't. The upshot of the investigation was that Judge Jenkins was dismissed from the bench for his misconduct and several other judges were suspended for their failure to speak up. In the meantime, Alex was pulling in as many retired judges as she could to keep the wheels of justice from completely falling off while her colleagues served their suspensions. Mrs. Jenkins came back from Florida long enough to file divorce proceedings and then promptly returned to Florida to let the lawyers fight it out. It was to be a short-lived fight.  Within two days a realtor's sign hung in the front yard of the ex-judge's home.

In the week before Thanksgiving, the trial team of Will, Luis, Rosalind, Jackie, and Liz met with Rosie, Jorge, and Yolanda in the big conference room at Johnston & Blackwell.  Of the thirteen million dollar settlement, the law firm received $4,333,333.00  to cover its fees and costs.  The rest of the money was divided up to provide 'up front' money so that Rosie and the kids could move into a comfortable home with plenty of room for all of them.  Education funds were set up for Jorge and Yolanda to make certain they would get the best education money could buy and an annuity was purchased for each that would pay out over their lifetimes.  A second annuity was purchased to provide Rosie with a monthly income that would comfortably take care of her for the rest of her life and allow her to stop working if that is what she chose.

The rest of the settlement was going into an Internal Revenue Service 501(c)(3) charitable nonprofit called the Felipe Ruiz Foundation.  Rosie and Jorge were to be two of the trustees and Yolanda would join them when she reached eighteen.  A third trustee came as a surprise to Will.  Ricky Storm, the guard at Northern who's life Felipe had saved, would also participate in the foundation.  Rosie explained that he had stayed in touch with her and her children from time to time and had always told her that he would help in any way he could because of what Felipe had done for him.  This seemed to her to be a good fit.  The purpose of the foundation was to provide assistance for young at-risk men and women in the greater Albuquerque area to help them avoid following Felipe's path or the path nearly taken by Jorge.  Will made a note to himself to talk with the firm about donating part of their fee from the case to the foundation.  It seemed like absolutely the right thing to do and, knowing Luis, he knew he already had one vote on his side.

Saying goodbye to Rosie and her family was especially hard for the trial team.  They had been through so much with the family that this closure after all the time that had passed wasn't easy.  Luis was the most emotional and cried openly as he hugged each of the family members.  They knew that they would stay in touch and that there would be more contact with Rosie and the foundation as time went on and that was a comfort to them.  Part of the upshot of the whole case was that the firm's plaintiff's practice had never been busier and there were plenty of matters in the pipeline to keep them busy.  Jorge promised Luis that he would stay in school and live his dream of becoming a lawyer one day.  Both Will and Luis encouraged him and both in the backs of their minds thought Jorge Herrera might well be the next generation at Johnston & Blackwell.

After the family left, Luis and Will had a moment alone.

"Luis, how are you feeling?"

"I feel good, Will.  Thanks.  Doctors say as long as I pace myself, they don't want to do anything like a bypass or stents or anything.  Just monitoring, some diet changes, exercise, stuff like that."

"Excellent, Luis, truly excellent."

Will walked down the hall to his office wondering again whether Luis had really had a heart attack or if this had been the biggest con Luis had ever pulled.  He smiled to himself.  Con or not, he was where he needed and wanted to be.

# CHAPTER TWENTY-EIGHT
## CONSTRUCTION PROJECT

Will got home before Alex that late afternoon, poured himself a Jameson's, and went out to the hot tub.  She was working more hours than ever simply trying to keep the court ahead of the increasing backlog of cases.  Even with as many retired judges as she could muster, the suspensions were still taking their toll.  Thank God they were only for 30 days.  She finally got home and joined him several minutes later.

"I've been thinking."  Never a good sign as a starter but he kept his mouth shut.

"I think we should put a shed over in the corner of the yard, right over there.  We're getting way too much stuff like garden tools, bikes, and the little closet in the carport is crammed.  I'm thinking we get somebody to do it right, like design and build it so it blends in with the rest of the townhouse.  Sound good?"

He thought about it for a minute and two things came to mind.  Yes, it was a very good idea and two, he would like to be the one to design and build it.  He ran that by Alex who raised an eyebrow.

"Will, as near as I can tell, you about killed yourself several times over when you were working with Rusty, and didn't succeed only because he wouldn't let you climb ladders and work with any power tools that could eviscerate you.  What are you thinking?"

"Alex, give me a chance.  I learned a lot and I'm a lot better than I was before.  Gimme a chance.  Whadda you say?"

He was sort of cute when he did that begging thing and she thought 'what the hell'.  They could always tear down what he started and get somebody good to do it right.  It wasn't like it was an emergency project or anything.

"Sure, Will, that would be great.  How long are you thinking it will take?"

"Lemme go get some paper and pencil and let's draw it out a little bit, OK?"  Will was already half out of the tub.

And so it began.  Trips to the hardware and lumber stores, purchases of a power saw and other tools, and Will was off to the races.  In the first part of December with Albuquerque enjoying a warm spell, he took three days off, and in three days put the entire project together from setting the flooring to constructing the walls and roof and framing all of it in.  Alex, who her own self was no slouch with a hammer, would come home each day and be stunned by the progress.  When she got home the third night it was completely finished and Will had bought a bottle of champagne to celebrate.

"Well, what do you think?"

"Will, it is absolutely beautiful to behold.  I am amazed at what you've done.  It is wonderful!"  She gave him a big kiss.  She walked around it in truth looking to see if it was indeed as good as it looked and again was stunned at the quality of the work.

"Probably shouldn't hit the champagne bottle against it for fear of it all coming down, should I?"

She laughed that laugh he loved so much.

"I don't want you breaking the bottle 'til we drink the champagne, Will.  Congratulations."

"Hey thanks.  Now take a picture with me in front of it so I can send it to Rusty and Dan, OK?"

"Sure."  She did and he emailed it to them.

The next morning, he heard back from both.

Dan: 'You and what army helped with that?'

Rusty: 'How many fingernails and how many 'shits'? Told you the Leatherman could do anything.'

It made his day.  Tomorrow the world.

Over the next several months, the investigation into the relationship between AAA Excavation and the state and federal agencies that awarded contracts continued even with the demise of Harry Conway and the demise of the company.  Indictments were ultimately returned against two state workers and one federal employee alleging that they had received thousands of dollars in kickbacks from Conway in exchange for letting contracts to AAA and looking the other way on the safety issues.  All three pled guilty ahead of trial and all three received prison sentences.

The mystery remained as to where the money had gone.  As a part of the investigation, they had looked at offshore accounts, Swiss accounts, and had combed every financial institution in the country looking for some connection between Conway, AAA Excavation, and the presumably hundreds of thousands if not millions of dollars that were missing.  Nothing.  They went back to his house and this time found the safe in his office that had been missed the first time.  But it was empty.

In the meantime, Margaret Espinoza continued her long slog back to normalcy.  Alex had dinner with her every so often and was pleased at how much better she was looking and feeling. The deaths of Conway, Crenshaw, Alright, and Baker were still open but, given the passage of time, the chances of solving them or even proving a connection between them became more and more remote.  The file was still on her desk but other fresher cases were pushing it farther and farther away.

On a whim one afternoon, she picked the file up and began to go through it one more time.  She reviewed the autopsy reports for Crenshaw, Alright, and Baker and, for the first time, noticed that three different pathologists had all noted an oddity in the knife wounds that had killed all three of them.  She read them each twice and then sat back and thought about it.  Each of the three doctors had noted that the wounds were smooth on one side but that, for Crenshaw and Baker, there was a tearing of the skin on the other edge as though the wounds had been made by a knife that had one smooth edge and one that was serrated.  Because Alright's throat had been cut, that wound was a clean cut except for one end that was torn and ragged near his left ear.  What was most important to her was that it could be the same knife and that would be the connection between at least the murders of Alright, Crenshaw, and Baker.  There was no way to tell about Conway because there was so little left of him, but it stood to reason that if the three crew chiefs were killed by the same weapon and the same person, his death must also be connected.

The detective felt that familiar rush of adrenalin when something like this happened and, per her custom, she put the file down to do something else and then come back to it.

When she picked it back up later that afternoon her conclusion was the same.  Three of the four had very likely been killed by the same knife.  The question remained:  who of all of the hundreds of people who had been abused by AAA Excavation had done it?

She got the AAA Excavation files out of the filing cabinet and began to go through the massive safety investigations, many of which hadn't even been started until after the Ruiz trial.  It was a tragedy beyond description of serious injury after serious injury after serious injury, none of which anybody with authority ever acted on.  The injured got worker's compensation benefits for as long as they were off, AAA paid ridiculous amounts for the coverage, and everybody turned the other way to the practices that were, at the very best, barbaric.  Besides Felipe Ruiz, there had been three other fatalities, one of which was another cave-in and two of which occurred when the men had been run over by machinery.  Any one of the employees or their family members could have been responsible for the killings of the AAA men.  Given what she had been through with her son's death, she could certainly empathize with whomever had done it, and that created a larger moral question for her.

What would she do if she did know who did it?

When Ronnie Espinoza's murderer had been arrested, Margaret had secretly planned his death and had gone over and over the scenario in her mind. She would make the son of a bitch pay with unimaginable suffering before she killed him. It hadn't gotten that far because the murderer had died of a catastrophic cardiac event but, even after his death, she still dreamed of what she would have done to him. And that was exactly what had been done to Harry Conway. A shiver went down her spine.

Four men didn't deserve to be murdered. By all accounts, they didn't deserve to live.

Just as she was pondering what to do next, her phone rang. Officers had just called in three gunshot fatalities in the War Zone, the same area of Albuquerque her son had been killed in. She threw the AAA Excavation files back in the cabinet, grabbed her coat and gun, and hurried for the door.

He was driving her crazy. Ever since the shed was finished, Will was thinking he was starring in some reality show like *This Old House.* He had turned the carport into a work room and was now in the process of fixing as many problems in the townhouse as he could find or make up. He had made built-in book cases over the holidays, reconfigured the kitchen by knocking out a wall, and now was contemplating adding a 'studio/office' off the back. One night he had even gone so far as to wonder out loud about building a house from scratch. Rusty had created a monster.

The suspensions of the judges had come and gone and life in the courthouse was back to normal. Alex had seen an announcement that former District Judge Donald Jenkins was opening a law office called Donald Jenkins & Associates, P.C. She found it hysterically funny because any time any lawyer ever put '…& Associates…' after their name, there weren't any. On the other hand, he had a good-sized client base built in because of all of the prostitutes he knew, so maybe he could make a living representing them and bartering for his services. 'Asshole' she muttered under her breath.

Will kept up with Rosie, Jorge, and Yolanda. They had bought a nice house with enough room for all three of them. Rosie continued to work at Garcia's even though she didn't have to, and when Will asked her about it, she just said, "It's who I am." Johnston & Blackwell had given $500,000 to the Felipe Ruiz Foundation and it was up and running.

One day in March, Will googled the Foundation and discovered that it had assets that were significantly more than the assets that had started the Foundation and the contribution from the firm. It stopped him in his tracks. There had been a lot of media exposure when the Foundation had been announced and both Will and Rosie had been interviewed at length about where the funds came from and what the purpose of the Foundation was. Will looked up the list of contributors. While there were some donors whose names were listed, the great majority of additional donors were anonymous and were in cash ranging from $5 to $25,000. He tried to figure out what to do with the information. He went to the one person he trusted more than anybody even in the worst of their times. His wife.

They met for lunch on a cold and rainy day which in Albuquerque was the talk of the town and which in Michigan would have been just one more cold and rainy day. She listened to her husband and she read the list of donors that he had printed off. She had the same question he did.

"Where did all that cash come from?"

"I have no idea but a bigger question is should I ask, and an even bigger question is do I want to know?"

Alex thought about it for a minute. "You really don't have any right to ask the question, I guess. You represented Felipe's Estate and that representation is over." She took another bite of her green chile cheeseburger. "So the Trustees of the Foundation could just tell you to pound sand. Everything on this list seems legitimate with the only weird things being how much is in cash and how much is anonymous. But you're right, it comes back to you - should you ask and do you want to know?"

"Here's what scares me, Alex. What if the money came from Harry Conway? Somebody killed him and somebody was in his house. What if it was Rosie?"

"I thought Jorge and Yolanda said she was home on the nights that Conway might have been killed."

"What if they're lying? What if she came home and then went out again? What if she didn't do it but she knows who did? If the money came from Conway, Rosie knows who killed him even if she didn't." He flashed to that look in her eyes months ago when Margaret Espinoza asked her if she had any other information about Conway's death.  Both Will and Rita Alvarson had noticed it.  Thank God Margaret hadn't.

"Here's the ultimate question.  Let's say you find out its Conway's money that is padding the Foundation's assets.  What do you do with that information?" They were silent for a minute.

"And Will, one more thing.  If you do find out, I don't want to know.  You okay with that?"

He nodded and picked up the check.

# CHAPTER THIRTY-ONE
## WILL AND JACKIE

It was a beautiful warm sunny day in Albuquerque in early April, the kind of day that people walk around in shorts and T-shirts and have the tops down on their convertibles.

Will asked Jackie if she wanted to get a sandwich and go to the park and have lunch. They got their orders from the deli, got to the park, and found a table. They exchanged small talk about Alex and Josephine and about some of the plaintiffs' cases that were coming into the firm.

"Amazing what an 18 million dollar verdict will do for public relations, isn't it, Will?"

"Amazing. Equally amazing what an incredible recovery Luis has made from his heart problems."

"Truly."

"Almost as though he never even had the heart attack at all."

"Pretty amazing, Will."

Jackie knew him well enough to know that Will hadn't asked her to lunch to make small talk about cases and Luis. She was pretty sure why they were there and as they were finishing up, he asked her.

"How much do you know, Jackie?"

She looked at him for a minute and thought about lying but that had never been her style.

"Some. Not all." She wondered if he would want to know what she knew.

"You, Jackie?"

"No, Will." Quiet and sure.

He felt a huge weight lift off his shoulders.

He nodded and looked at his watch. "Time to head back to the grind, doncha think?"

"Sounds good. Hey and thanks for lunch."

On their way back to the office, he turned to her.

"I want to ask you one thing."

"Okay."

"Justice?"

"Yes."

"Then that's all I need."  And then as much to himself as to Jackie, "'Cause the law's not always or even most of the time about seeking truth.  But it's all about seeking justice."

Jackie LaPointe knew the difference.

They were on their way home on I-40 when they passed the massive billboard advertising the services of Donald Jenkins and Associates, Attorneys at Law, *Serving the Underserved – Free Consultation* and both of them started laughing at the same time. They had heard through the grapevine that he actually was doing quite well serving the underserved with his primary client base the prostitutes and pimps of East Central, a place he knew so well. His cases were all in the Metropolitan Court, a step below District Court, and his path never crossed either Alex's or Will's. Just as well, but even Will wished him no ill will, at least not a lot. He had paid the price.

The murders of the four AAA Excavation men were never solved and the cases were relegated to the Cold Case Division of the Bernalillo County Sheriff's Department and the Albuquerque Police Department. A better description should have been the Very Cold Case Division because solving those murders was not anybody's priority.

The Felipe Ruiz Foundation continued to prosper although Will noticed that anonymous cash donations had decreased and more traditional donations had increased significantly as the foundation gained traction in the community.

In early May, Will, Rosalind, Jackie, and Liz were invited to a 'private party' at Rosie Ruiz' new home. When they got there, Rosie, Jorge, Yolanda, and Ricky Storm greeted them with the news that Ricky and Rosie had been married that morning in Santa Fe. There were champagne toasts and much hugging among everybody. At some point, Will needed to get rid of some champagne, found the main bathroom occupied, and went into the master bedroom and adjoining bathroom. On his way out, he noticed a knife on the dresser and picked it up. It was smooth and

sharp on one side of the blade and serrated on the other.  He looked
at it, hefted it, and thought it would be a good addition for his tool
box.  He would look for one the next time he was in one of the box
stores and he put the knife back where he found it.  Upon his return
to the living room, cake and coffee were being served and the
happiness and warmth were palpable.  It was a very special time
with the new family and, when they left, there were promises to
continue to get together.  Will commented on the way back to the
office that Rosie looked so much better and got total agreement
from the other three.  For some reason that Will couldn't fathom,
he made the conscious decision not to tell Alex about Rosie and
Ricky.  Maybe it was that look months ago that had crossed
Rosie's face when Detective Espinoza had asked Rosie whether
she knew of anybody who might have killed Harry Conway.  Or
maybe not.

Over Memorial Day, Alex and Will got back to Michigan
to get the lake house open.  It was the first time Alex had been
back in well over a year and she was concerned about the reaction
she might get from Reba Sue.  She needn't have worried.  She was
met with fresh eggs from the chicken coop and a fish fry made up
of blue gills and perch caught over the winter by Rusty.  Grace
joined them for a couple of days and all was well with her.  Robert
had called and accepted the invitation for his family to come for
the July Fourth weekend and stay for as long as they could.

On Sunday morning, Will got up ahead of Alex and Grace
and went for a walk along the beach.  It was chilly but sunny and
he marveled at the freshness that each new spring brings to the lake
shore.  He had come to love Albuquerque and the high desert of
New Mexico but Michigan would always be his home.  His mind
wandered over the last months and all that had happened.  Alex
and Will had been through so much in their relationship almost
from the beginning and he was thrilled beyond measure that they
had survived together once again.  He lived in the now as much as

he could but wondered about the future and hoped that maybe all that had happened to them over the last several years was finally over and that they could finally enjoy some peace.

It was a good thing he didn't know the future.

# ABOUT THE AUTHOR

Bill Jack is a lawyer in West Michigan and he and his wife, Rebecca Sitterly, who is also the artist for the covers of all of the books, divide their time between Grand Rapids and Frog's Reach Farm in Montague.

www.ingramcontent.com/pod-product-compliance
Lightning Source LLC
Chambersburg PA
CBHW060803210726
48292CB00013B/1744